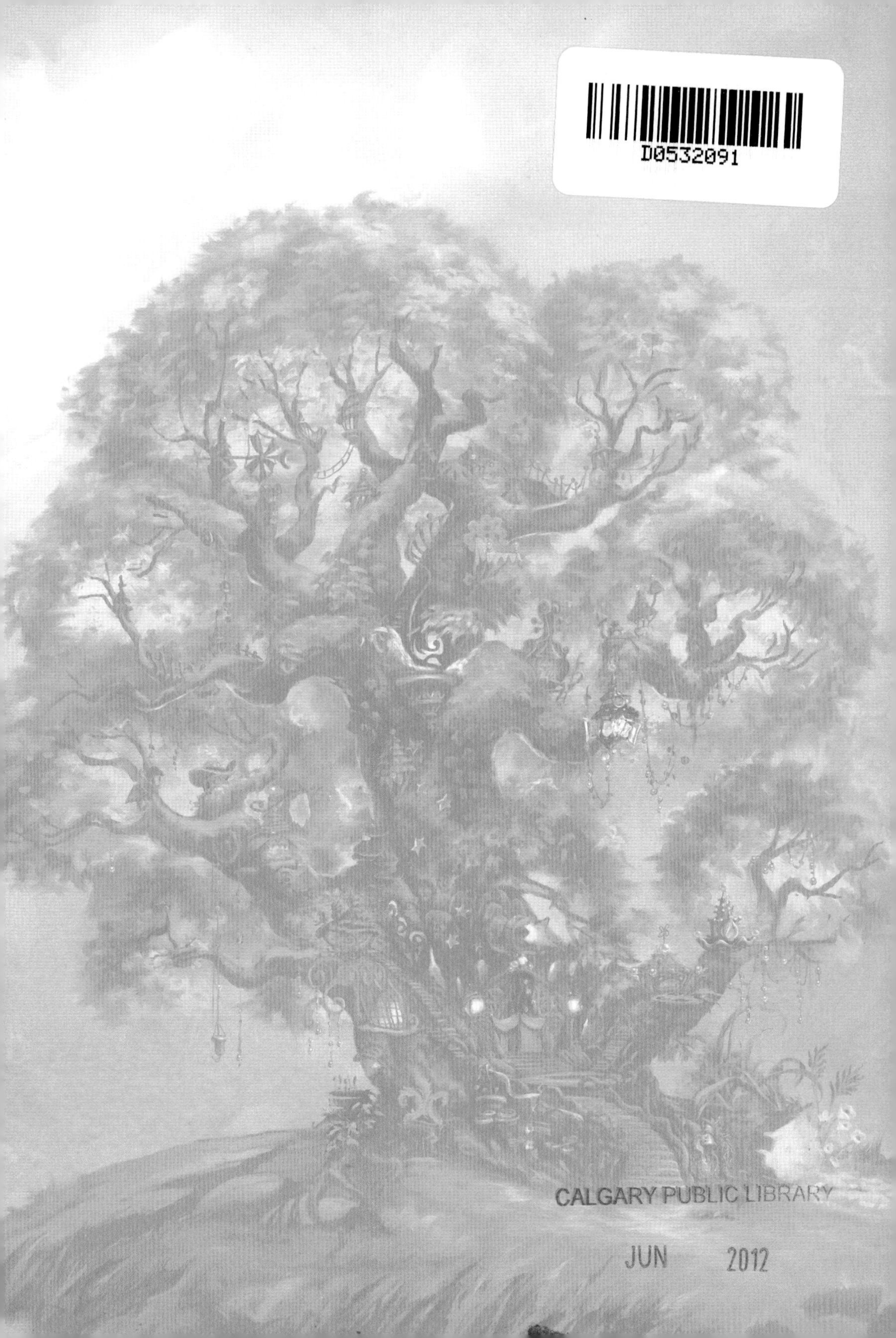

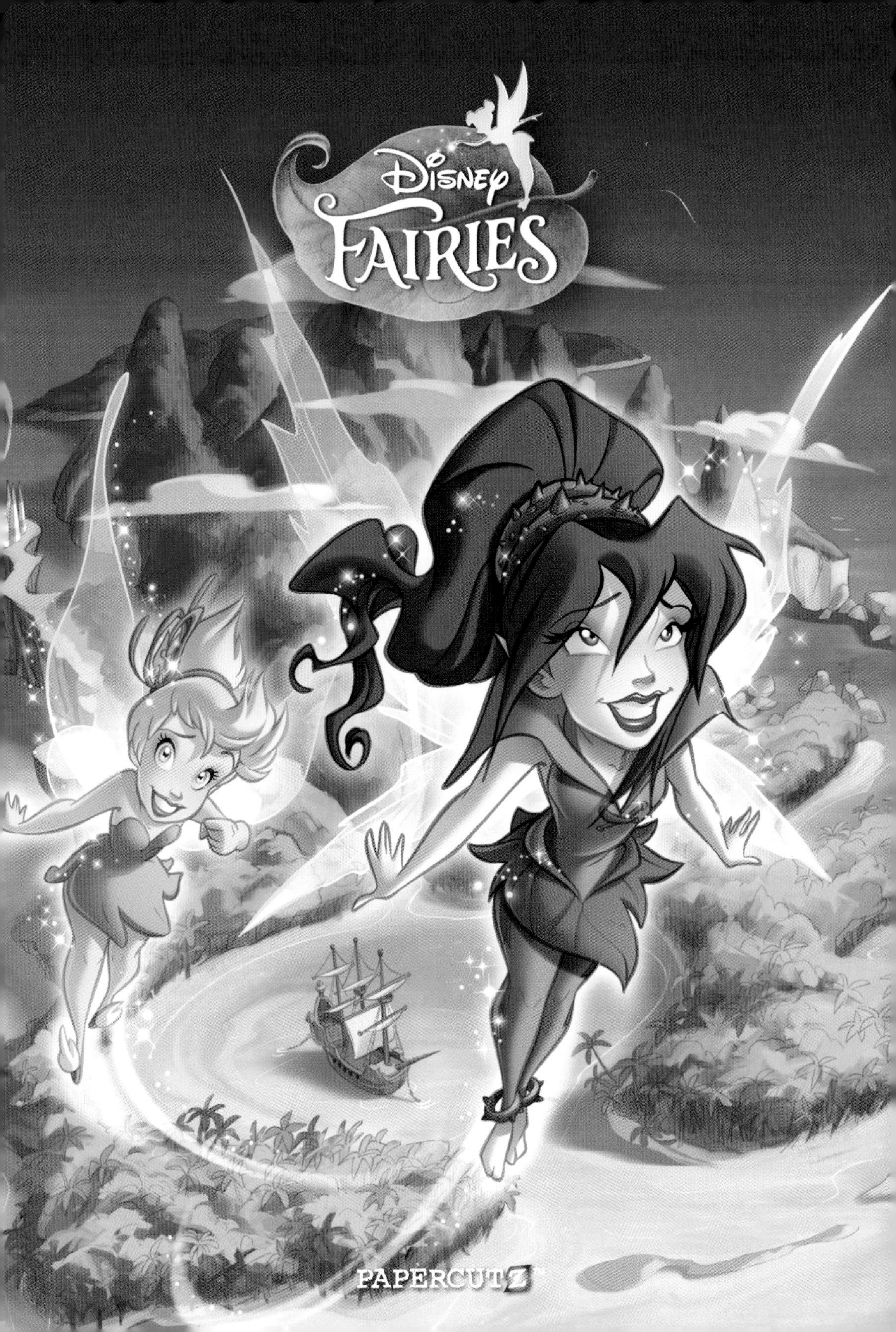
Disney
FAIRIES
PAPERCUTZ

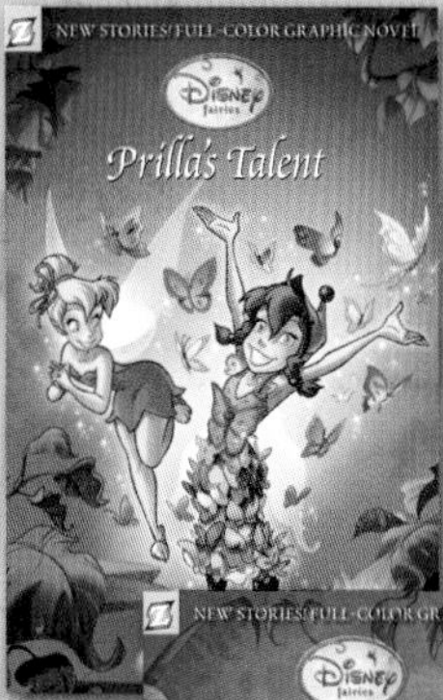
NEW STORIES! FULL-COLOR GRAPHIC NOVEL
Disney fairies
Prilla's Talent

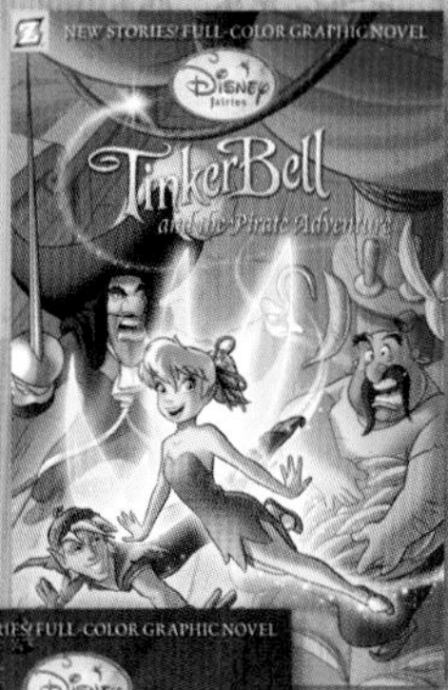
NEW STORIES! FULL-COLOR GRAPHIC NOVEL
Disney fairies
TinkerBell
and the Pirate Adventure

DISNEY FAIRIES

Graphic Novels Available from PAPERCUTZ

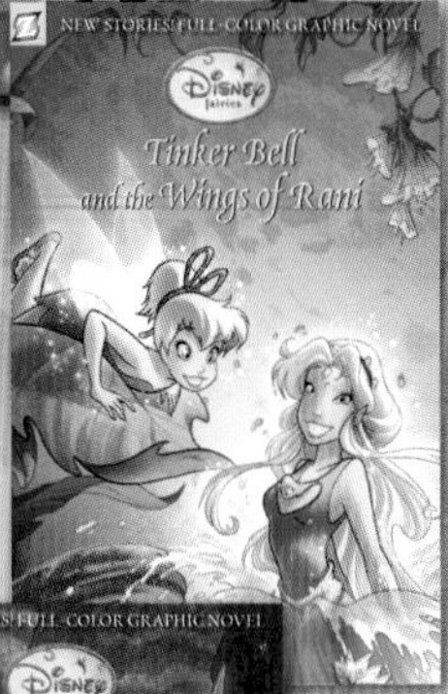
NEW STORIES! FULL-COLOR GRAPHIC NOVEL
Disney fairies
Tinker Bell
and the Wings of Rani

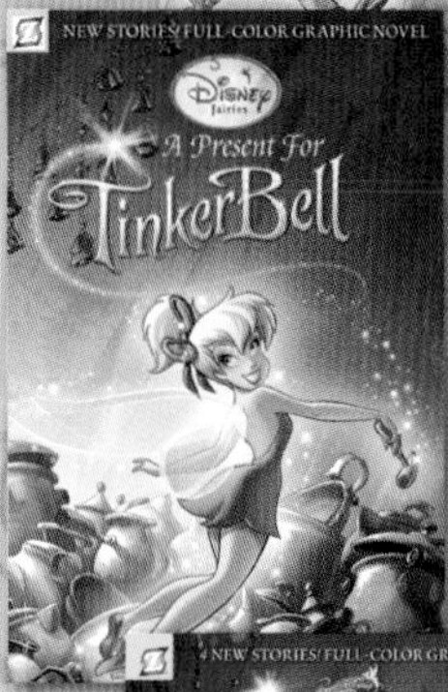
NEW STORIES! FULL-COLOR GRAPHIC NOVEL
Disney fairies
A Present For
TinkerBell

Graphic Novel #1
"Prilla's Talent"

Graphic Novel #2
"Tinker Bell and
the Wings of Rani"

Graphic Novel #3
"Tinker Bell and the Day of the Dragon"

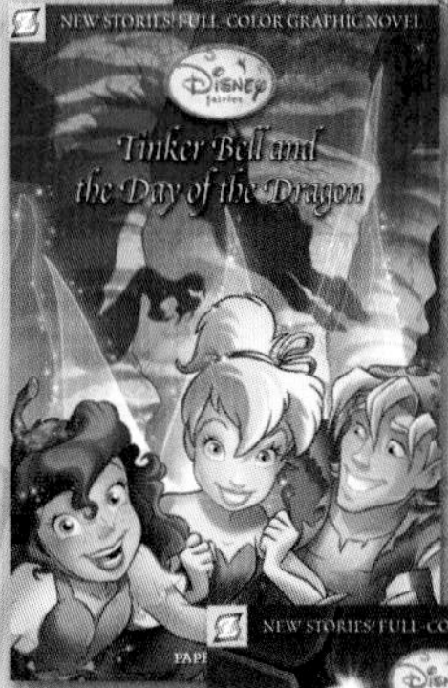
NEW STORIES! FULL-COLOR GRAPHIC NOVEL
Disney fairies
Tinker Bell and
the Day of the Dragon

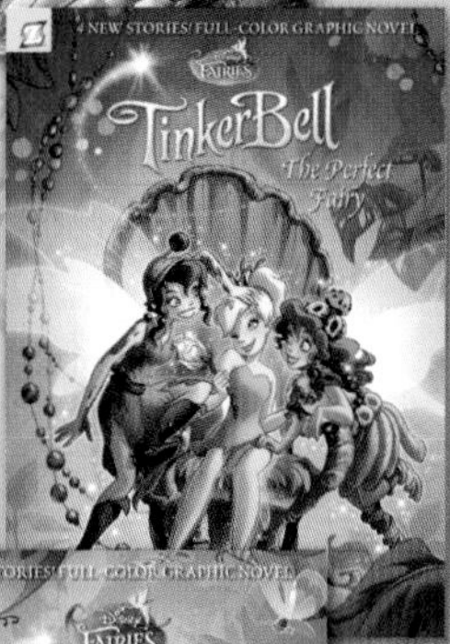
NEW STORIES! FULL-COLOR GRAPHIC NOVEL
Disney FAIRIES
TinkerBell
The Perfect Fairy

Graphic Novel #4
"Tinker Bell to the Rescue"

Graphic Novel #5
"Tinker Bell and
the Pirate Adventure"

Graphic Novel #6
"A Present for Tinker Bell"

Graphic Novel #7
"Tinker Bell the Perfect Fairy"

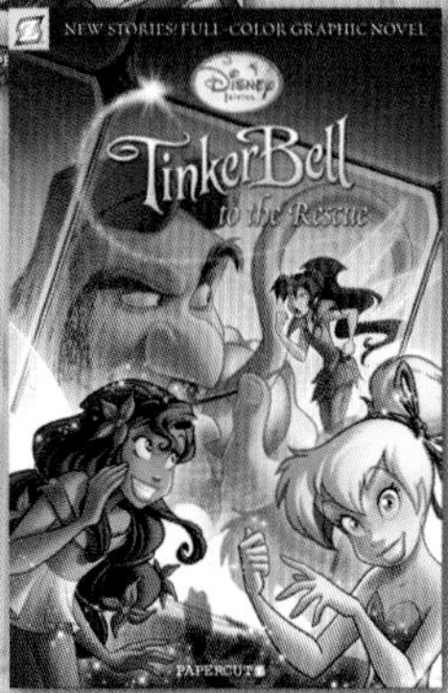
NEW STORIES! FULL-COLOR GRAPHIC NOVEL
Disney fairies
TinkerBell
to the Rescue
PAPERCUTZ

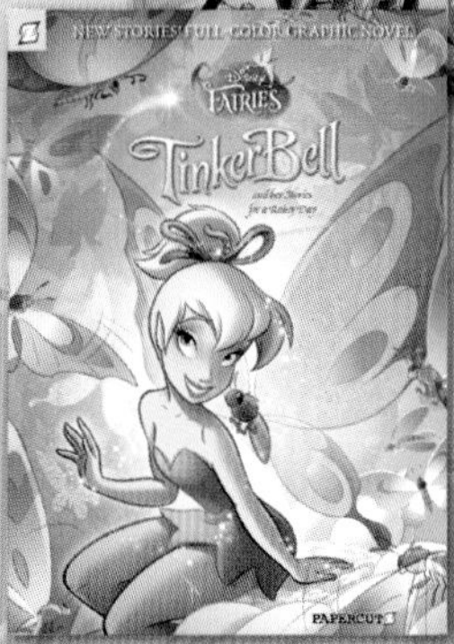
NEW STORIES! FULL-COLOR GRAPHIC NOVEL
Disney FAIRIES
TinkerBell
PAPERCUTZ

Coming Soon:
Graphic Novel #8
"Tinker Bell and her Stories
for a Rainy Day"

DISNEY FAIRIES graphic novels are available in paperback for $7.99 each;
in hardcover for $12.99 each except #5, $6.99PB, $10.99HC.
#6-8 are $7.99PB $11.99HC. Available at booksellers everywhere.

See more at www.papercutz.com

Or you can order from us: please add $4.00 for postage and handling for first book, and add $1.00 for each additional book. Please make check payable to NBM Publishing. Send to: Papercutz, 40 Exchange Place, Suite 1308, New York, NY 10005 or call 800 886 1223 (9-6 EST M-F) MC-Visa-Amex accepted.

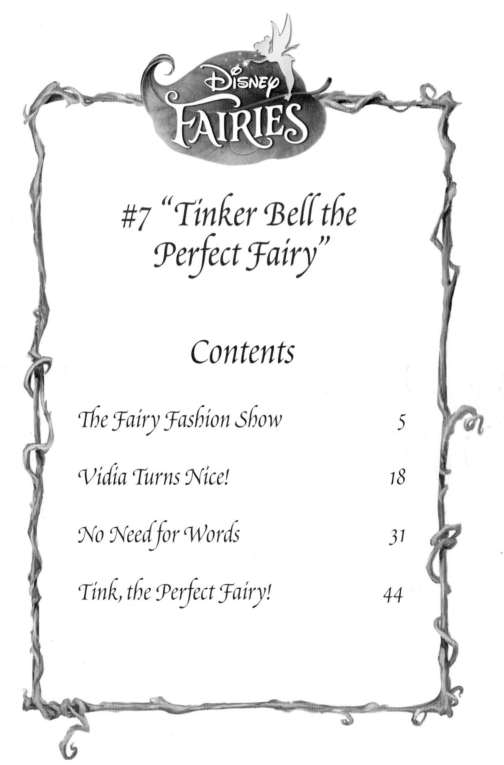

Disney FAIRIES

#7 "Tinker Bell the Perfect Fairy"

Contents

PAPERCUTZ™
NEW YORK

"The Fairy Fashion Show"
Script: Paola Mulazzi
Revised Dialogue: Cortney Faye Powell
Pencils: Andrea Greppi
Inks: Marina Baggio
Color: Stefania Santi
Letters: Lea Hernandez
Page 5 Art:
Pencils: Caterina Giogetti
Inks: Roberta Zanotta
Color: Andrea Cagol

"No Need for Words"
Script: Paola Mulazzi
Revised Dialogue: Cortney Faye Powell
Pencils: Antonello Dalena & Manuela Razzi
Inks: Marina Baggio
Color: Stefania Santi
Letters: Lea Hernandez
Page 31 Art:
Pencils: Andrea Greppi
Inks: Roberta Zanotta
Color: Andrea Cagol

"Vidia Turns Nice!"
Script: Paola Mulazzi
Revised Dialogue: Cortney Faye Powell
Pencils: Caterina Giorgetti
Inks: Roberta Zanotta
Color: Stefania Santi
Letters: Lea Hernandez
Page 18 Art:
Pencils: Emilio Urbano and Manuela
Razzi
Inks: Marina Baggio
Color: Andrea Cagol

"Tink, the Perfect Fairy!"
Script: Paola Mulazzi
Revised Dialogue: Cortney Faye Powell
Pencils: Antonello Dalena and Manuela Razzi
Inks: Marina Baggio
Color: Stefania Santi
Letters: Lea Hernandez
Page 44 Art:
Pencils: Caterina Giorgetti
Inks: Roberta Zanotta
Color: Andrea Cagol

Nelson Design Group – Production
Special Thanks – Jesse Post and Shiho Tilley
Michael Petranek – Associate Editor
Jim Salicrup – Editor-in-Chief

ISBN: 978-1-59707-281-6 paperback edition
ISBN: 978-1-59707-282-3 hardcover edition

Printed in Singapore. November 2011
by Tien Wah Press PTE LTD
4 Pandan Crescent
Singapore 128475

Distributed by Macmillan.

First Papercutz Printing

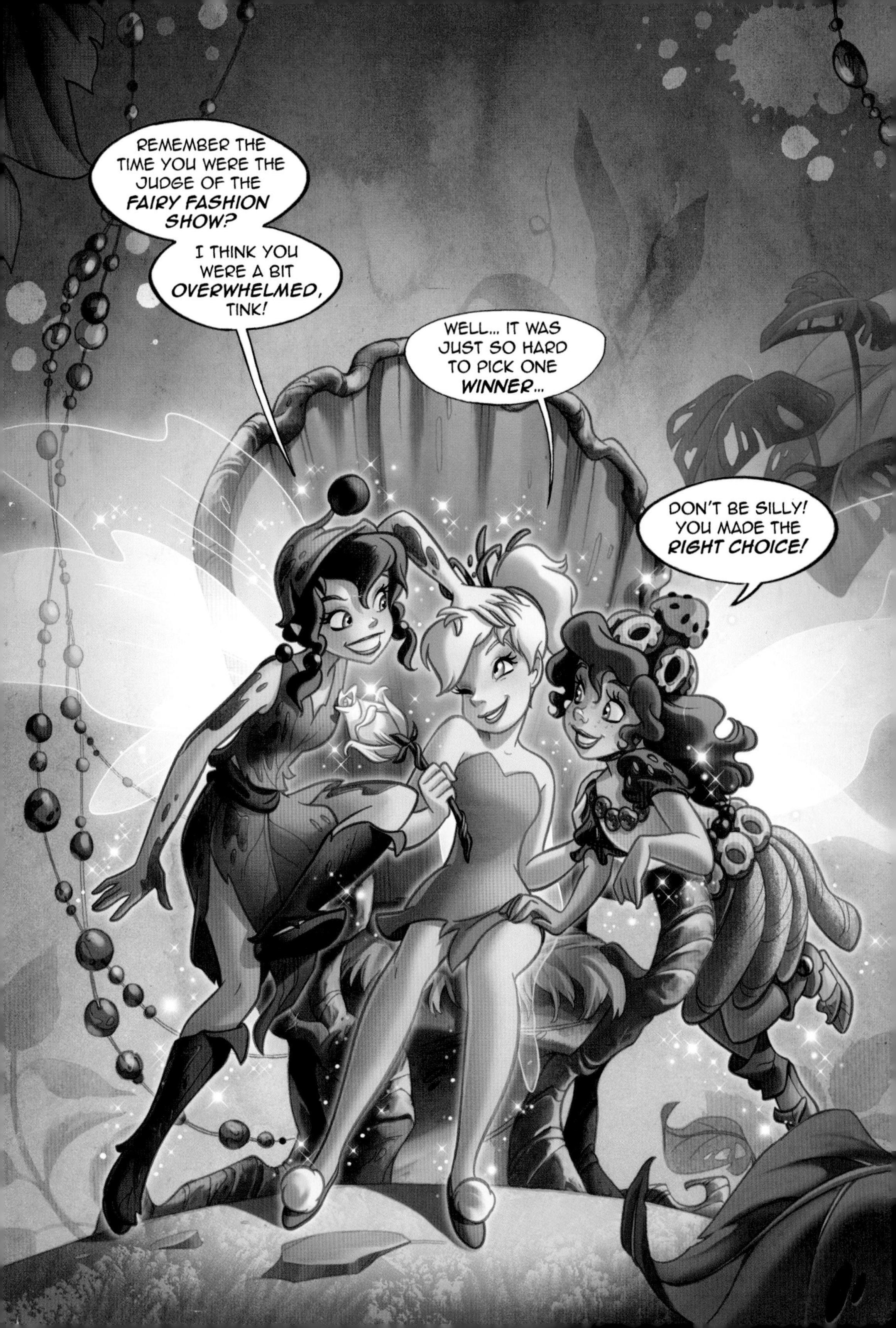
REMEMBER THE TIME YOU WERE THE JUDGE OF THE FAIRY FASHION SHOW?
I THINK YOU WERE A BIT OVERWHELMED, TINK!
WELL... IT WAS JUST SO HARD TO PICK ONE WINNER...
DON'T BE SILLY! YOU MADE THE RIGHT CHOICE!

Tinker Bell and the Fairy Fashion Show

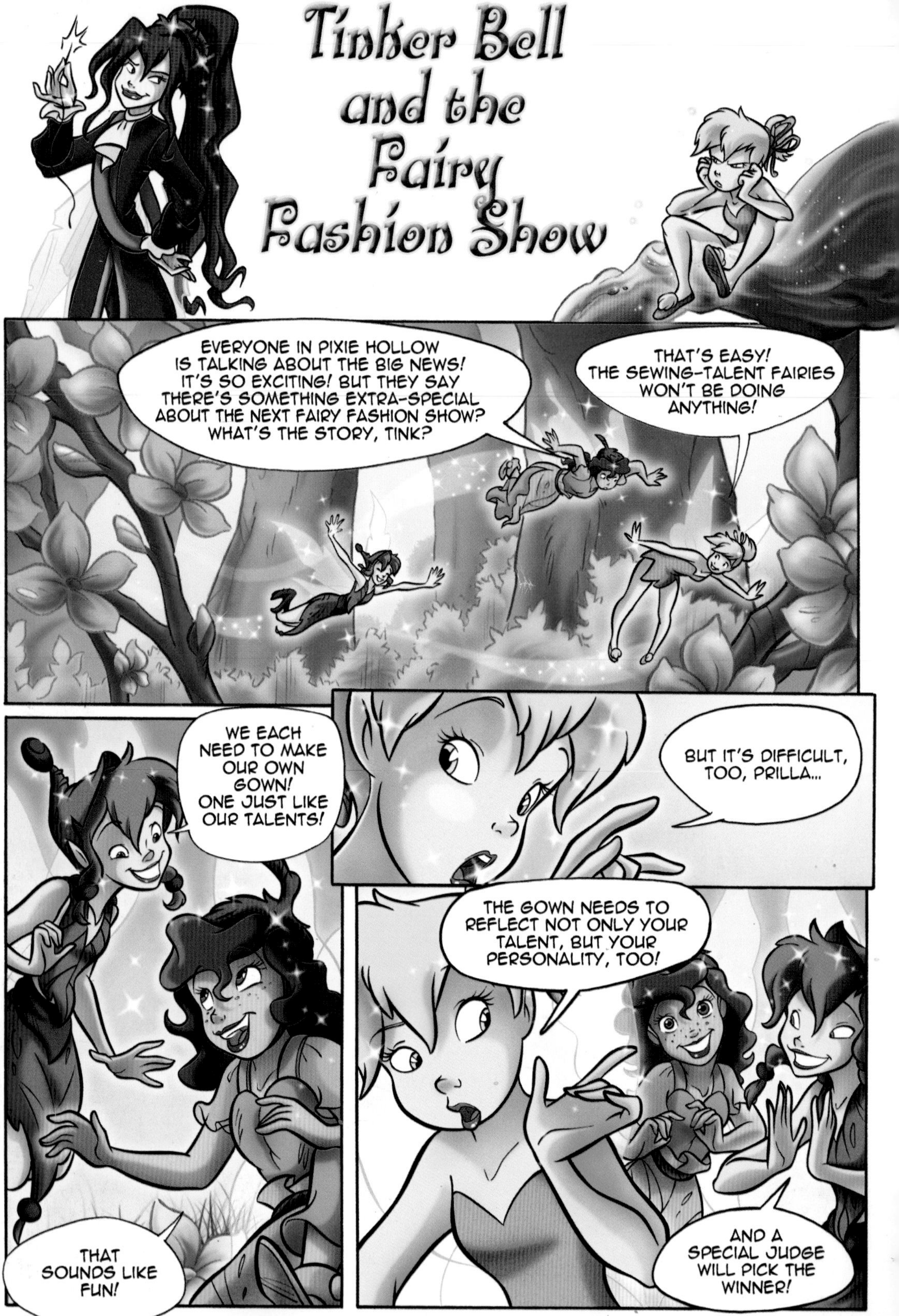

EVERYONE IN PIXIE HOLLOW IS TALKING ABOUT THE BIG NEWS! IT'S SO EXCITING! BUT THEY SAY THERE'S SOMETHING EXTRA-SPECIAL ABOUT THE NEXT FAIRY FASHION SHOW? WHAT'S THE STORY, TINK?
THAT'S EASY! THE SEWING-TALENT FAIRIES WON'T BE DOING ANYTHING!
WE EACH NEED TO MAKE OUR OWN GOWN! ONE JUST LIKE OUR TALENTS!
THAT SOUNDS LIKE FUN!
BUT IT'S DIFFICULT, TOO, PRILLA...
THE GOWN NEEDS TO REFLECT NOT ONLY YOUR TALENT, BUT YOUR PERSONALITY, TOO!
AND A SPECIAL JUDGE WILL PICK THE WINNER!

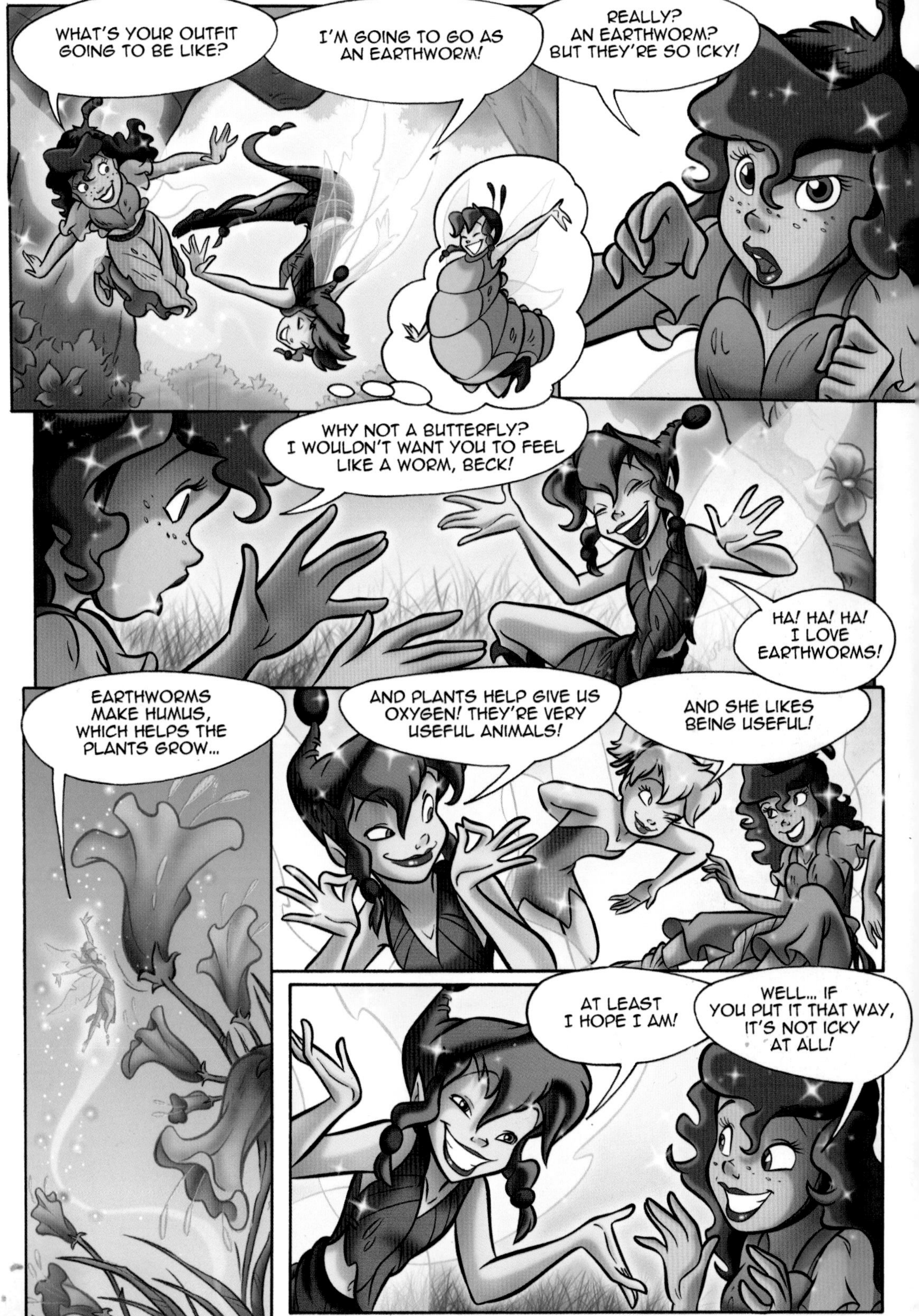
WHAT'S YOUR OUTFIT GOING TO BE LIKE?
I'M GOING TO GO AS AN EARTHWORM!
REALLY? AN EARTHWORM? BUT THEY'RE SO ICKY!
WHY NOT A BUTTERFLY? I WOULDN'T WANT YOU TO FEEL LIKE A WORM, BECK!
HA! HA! HA! I LOVE EARTHWORMS!
EARTHWORMS MAKE HUMUS, WHICH HELPS THE PLANTS GROW...
AND PLANTS HELP GIVE US OXYGEN! THEY'RE VERY USEFUL ANIMALS!
AND SHE LIKES BEING USEFUL!
AT LEAST I HOPE I AM!
WELL... IF YOU PUT IT THAT WAY, IT'S NOT ICKY AT ALL!

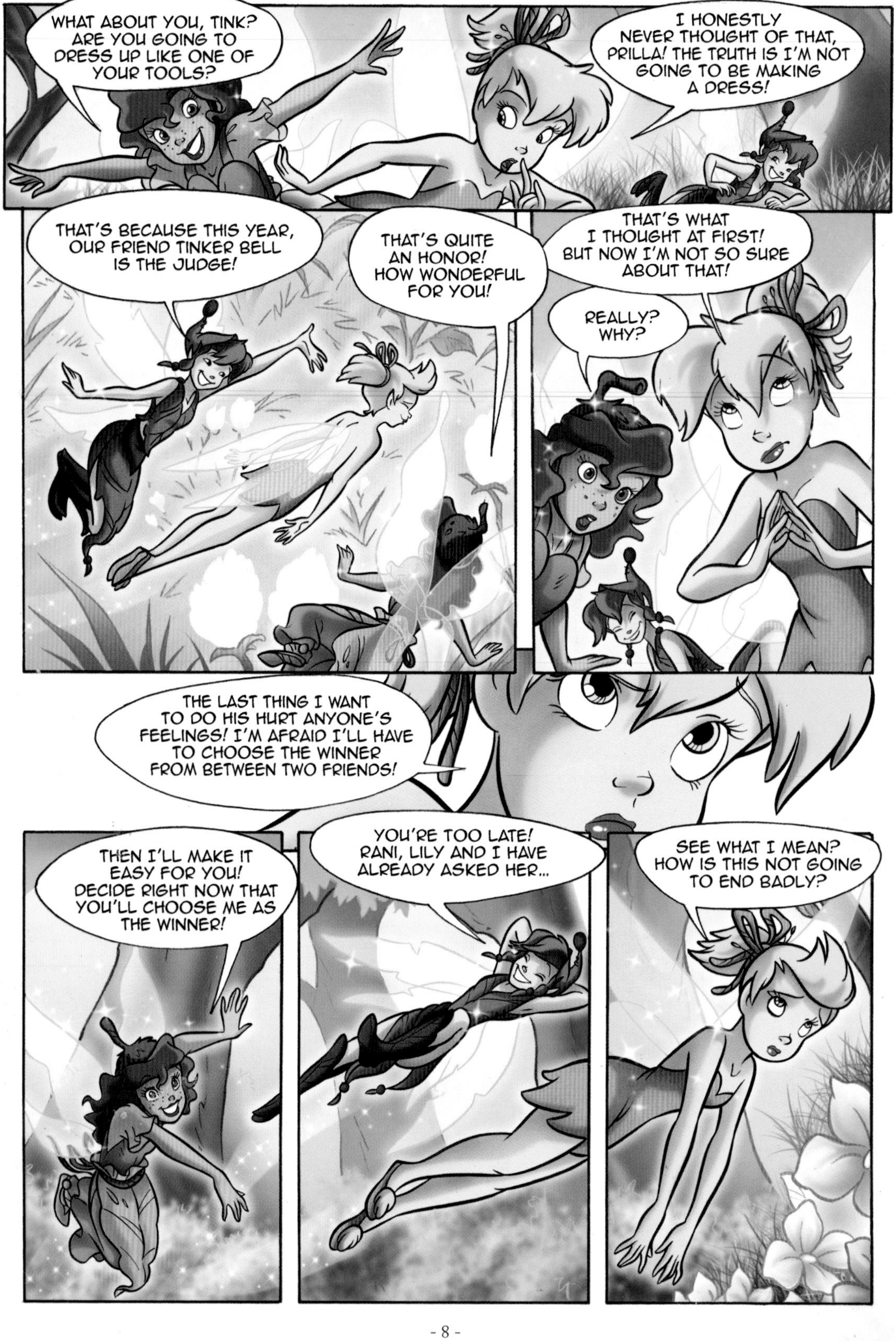

WHAT ABOUT YOU, TINK? ARE YOU GOING TO DRESS UP LIKE ONE OF YOUR TOOLS?
I HONESTLY NEVER THOUGHT OF THAT, PRILLA! THE TRUTH IS I'M NOT GOING TO BE MAKING A DRESS!
THAT'S BECAUSE THIS YEAR, OUR FRIEND TINKER BELL IS THE JUDGE!
THAT'S QUITE AN HONOR! HOW WONDERFUL FOR YOU!
THAT'S WHAT I THOUGHT AT FIRST! BUT NOW I'M NOT SO SURE ABOUT THAT!
REALLY? WHY?
THE LAST THING I WANT TO DO HIS HURT ANYONE'S FEELINGS! I'M AFRAID I'LL HAVE TO CHOOSE THE WINNER FROM BETWEEN TWO FRIENDS!
THEN I'LL MAKE IT EASY FOR YOU! DECIDE RIGHT NOW THAT YOU'LL CHOOSE ME AS THE WINNER!
YOU'RE TOO LATE! RANI, LILY AND I HAVE ALREADY ASKED HER...
SEE WHAT I MEAN? HOW IS THIS NOT GOING TO END BADLY?

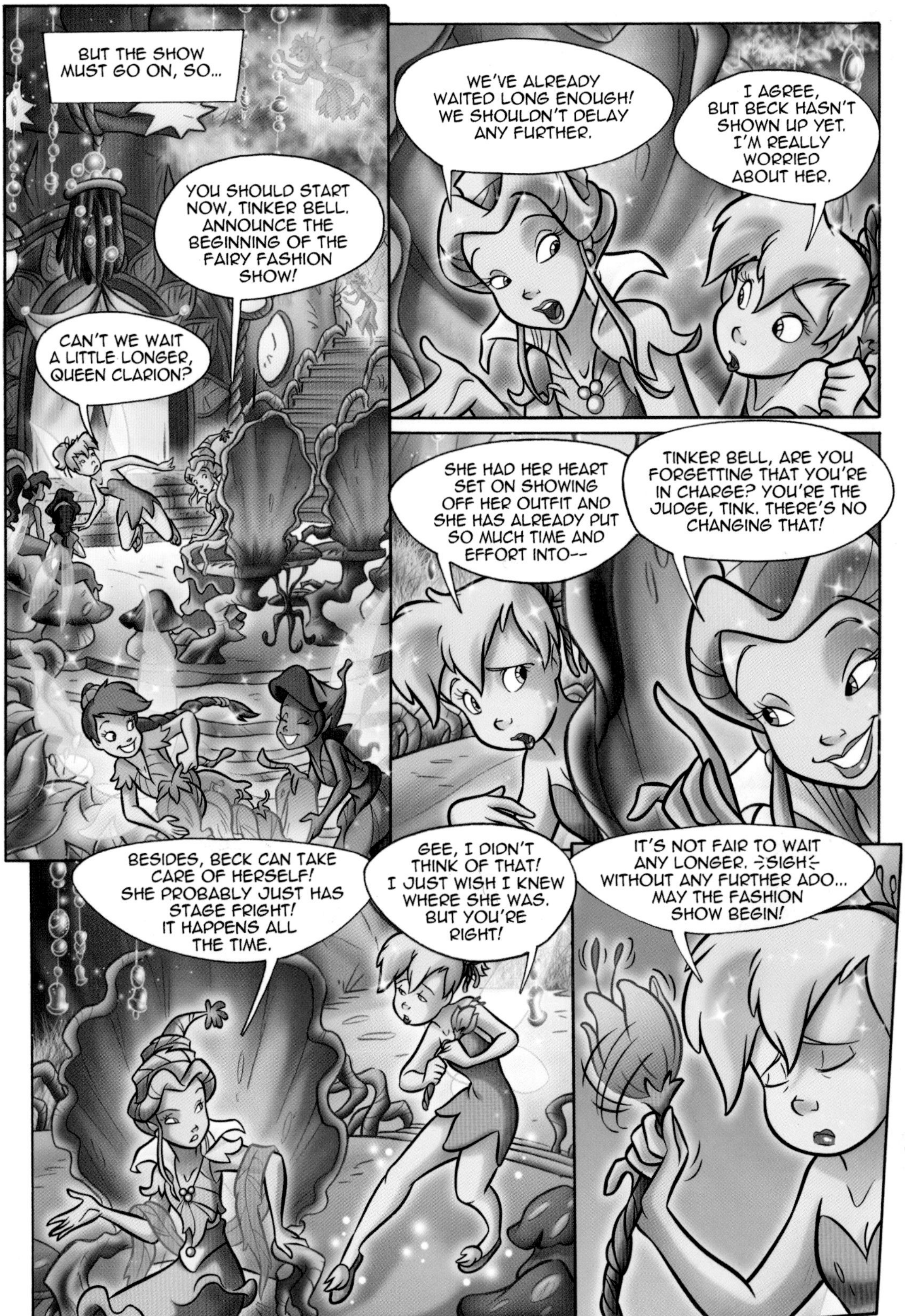
BUT THE SHOW MUST GO ON, SO...
YOU SHOULD START NOW, TINKER BELL. ANNOUNCE THE BEGINNING OF THE FAIRY FASHION SHOW!
CAN'T WE WAIT A LITTLE LONGER, QUEEN CLARION?
WE'VE ALREADY WAITED LONG ENOUGH! WE SHOULDN'T DELAY ANY FURTHER.
I AGREE, BUT BECK HASN'T SHOWN UP YET. I'M REALLY WORRIED ABOUT HER.
SHE HAD HER HEART SET ON SHOWING OFF HER OUTFIT AND SHE HAS ALREADY PUT SO MUCH TIME AND EFFORT INTO--
TINKER BELL, ARE YOU FORGETTING THAT YOU'RE IN CHARGE? YOU'RE THE JUDGE, TINK. THERE'S NO CHANGING THAT!
BESIDES, BECK CAN TAKE CARE OF HERSELF! SHE PROBABLY JUST HAS STAGE FRIGHT! IT HAPPENS ALL THE TIME.
GEE, I DIDN'T THINK OF THAT! I JUST WISH I KNEW WHERE SHE WAS. BUT YOU'RE RIGHT!
IT'S NOT FAIR TO WAIT ANY LONGER. SIGH WITHOUT ANY FURTHER ADO... MAY THE FASHION SHOW BEGIN!

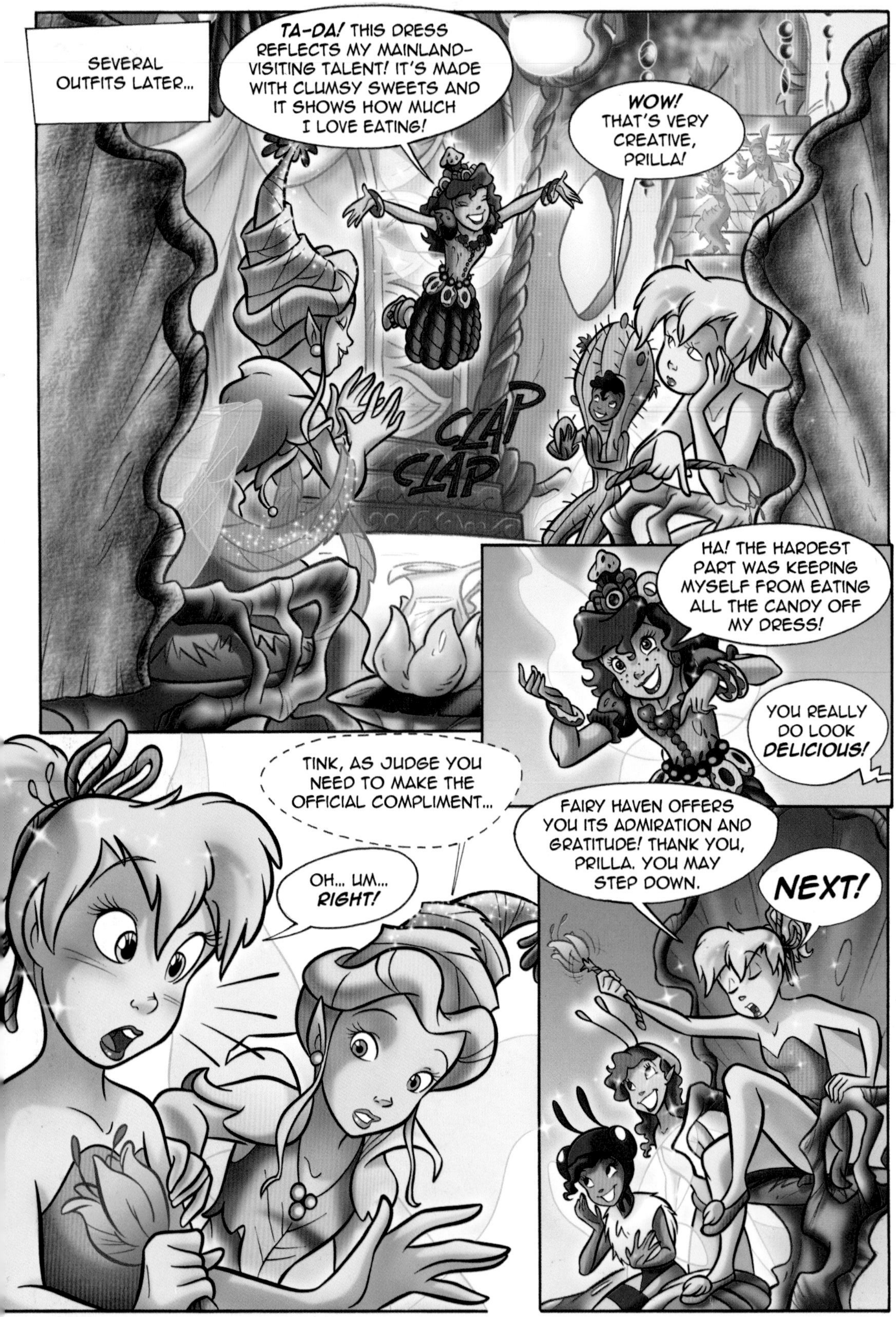
SEVERAL OUTFITS LATER...
TA-DA! THIS DRESS REFLECTS MY MAINLAND-VISITING TALENT! IT'S MADE WITH CLUMSY SWEETS AND IT SHOWS HOW MUCH I LOVE EATING!
WOW! THAT'S VERY CREATIVE, PRILLA!
CLAP CLAP
HA! THE HARDEST PART WAS KEEPING MYSELF FROM EATING ALL THE CANDY OFF MY DRESS!
YOU REALLY DO LOOK DELICIOUS!
TINK, AS JUDGE YOU NEED TO MAKE THE OFFICIAL COMPLIMENT...
OH... UM... RIGHT!
FAIRY HAVEN OFFERS YOU ITS ADMIRATION AND GRATITUDE! THANK YOU, PRILLA. YOU MAY STEP DOWN.
NEXT!

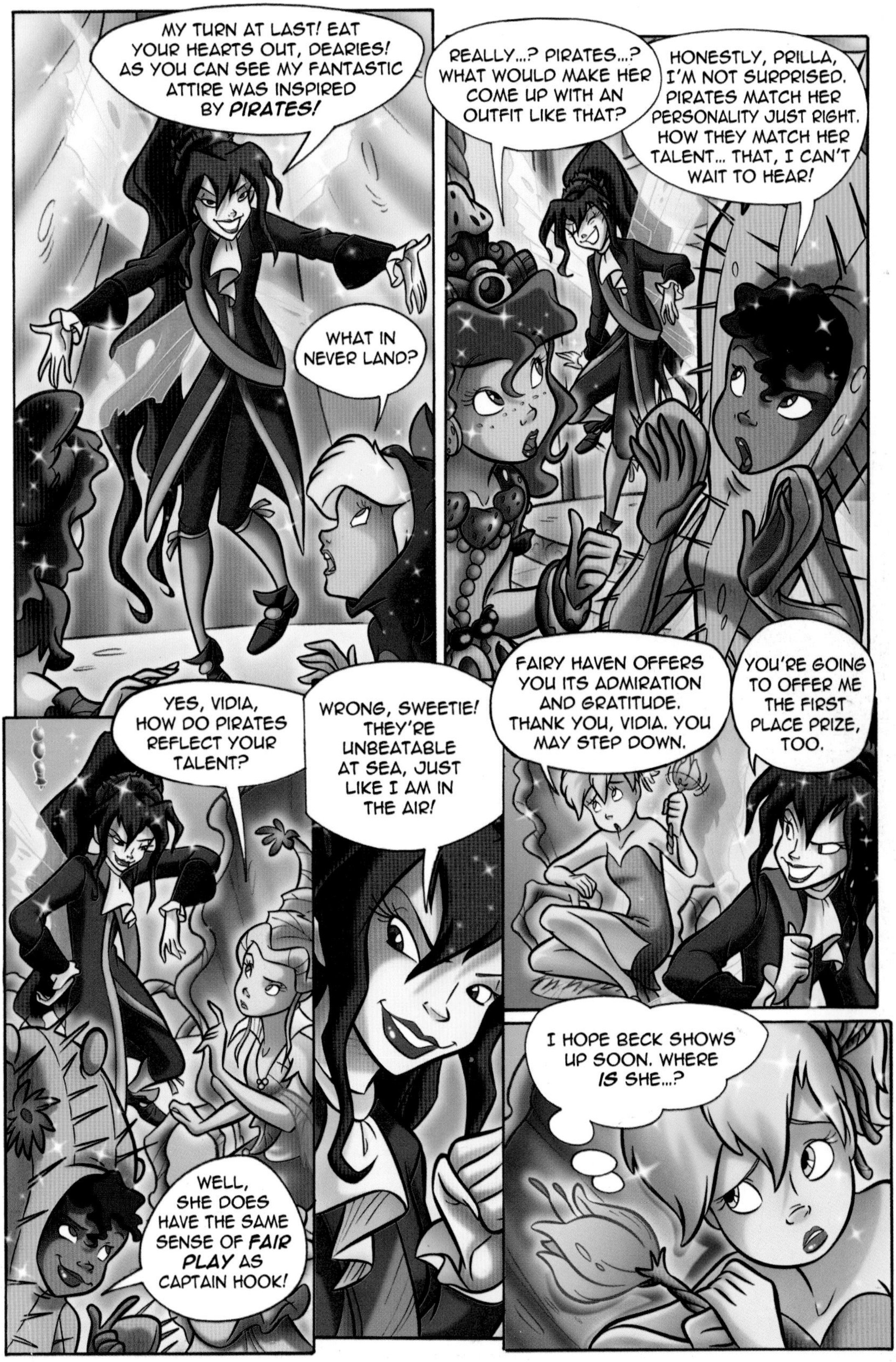
MY TURN AT LAST! EAT YOUR HEARTS OUT, DEARIES! AS YOU CAN SEE MY FANTASTIC ATTIRE WAS INSPIRED BY *PIRATES!*
WHAT IN NEVER LAND?
REALLY...? PIRATES...? WHAT WOULD MAKE HER COME UP WITH AN OUTFIT LIKE THAT?
HONESTLY, PRILLA, I'M NOT SURPRISED. PIRATES MATCH HER PERSONALITY JUST RIGHT. HOW THEY MATCH HER TALENT... THAT, I CAN'T WAIT TO HEAR!
YES, VIDIA, HOW DO PIRATES REFLECT YOUR TALENT?
WELL, SHE DOES HAVE THE SAME SENSE OF *FAIR PLAY* AS CAPTAIN HOOK!
WRONG, SWEETIE! THEY'RE UNBEATABLE AT SEA, JUST LIKE I AM IN THE AIR!
FAIRY HAVEN OFFERS YOU ITS ADMIRATION AND GRATITUDE. THANK YOU, VIDIA. YOU MAY STEP DOWN.
YOU'RE GOING TO OFFER ME THE FIRST PLACE PRIZE, TOO.
I HOPE BECK SHOWS UP SOON. WHERE *IS* SHE...?

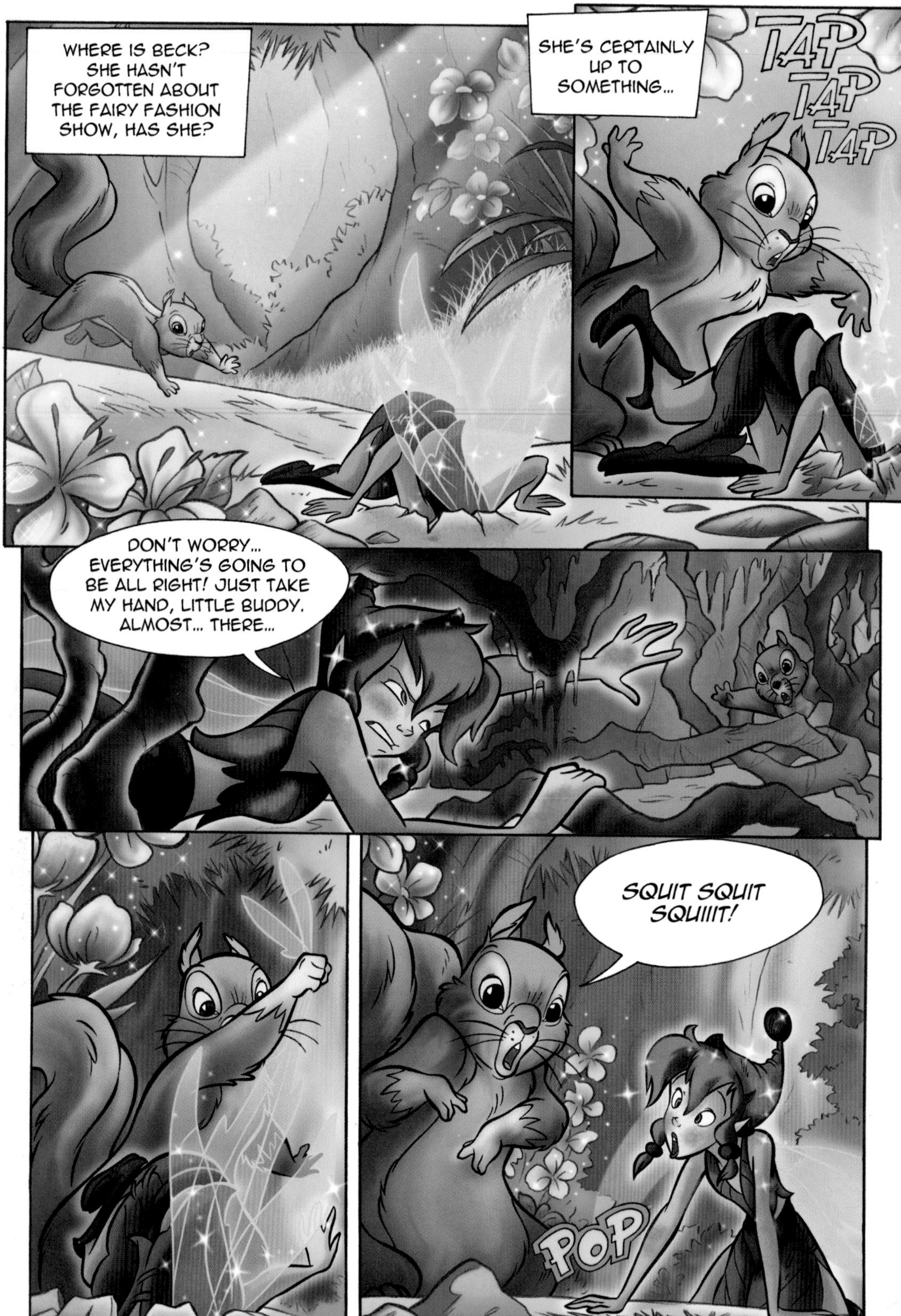
WHERE IS BECK? SHE HASN'T FORGOTTEN ABOUT THE FAIRY FASHION SHOW, HAS SHE?
SHE'S CERTAINLY UP TO SOMETHING...
TAP
TAP
TAP
DON'T WORRY... EVERYTHING'S GOING TO BE ALL RIGHT! JUST TAKE MY HAND, LITTLE BUDDY. ALMOST... THERE...
SQUIT SQUIT SQUIIIT!
POP

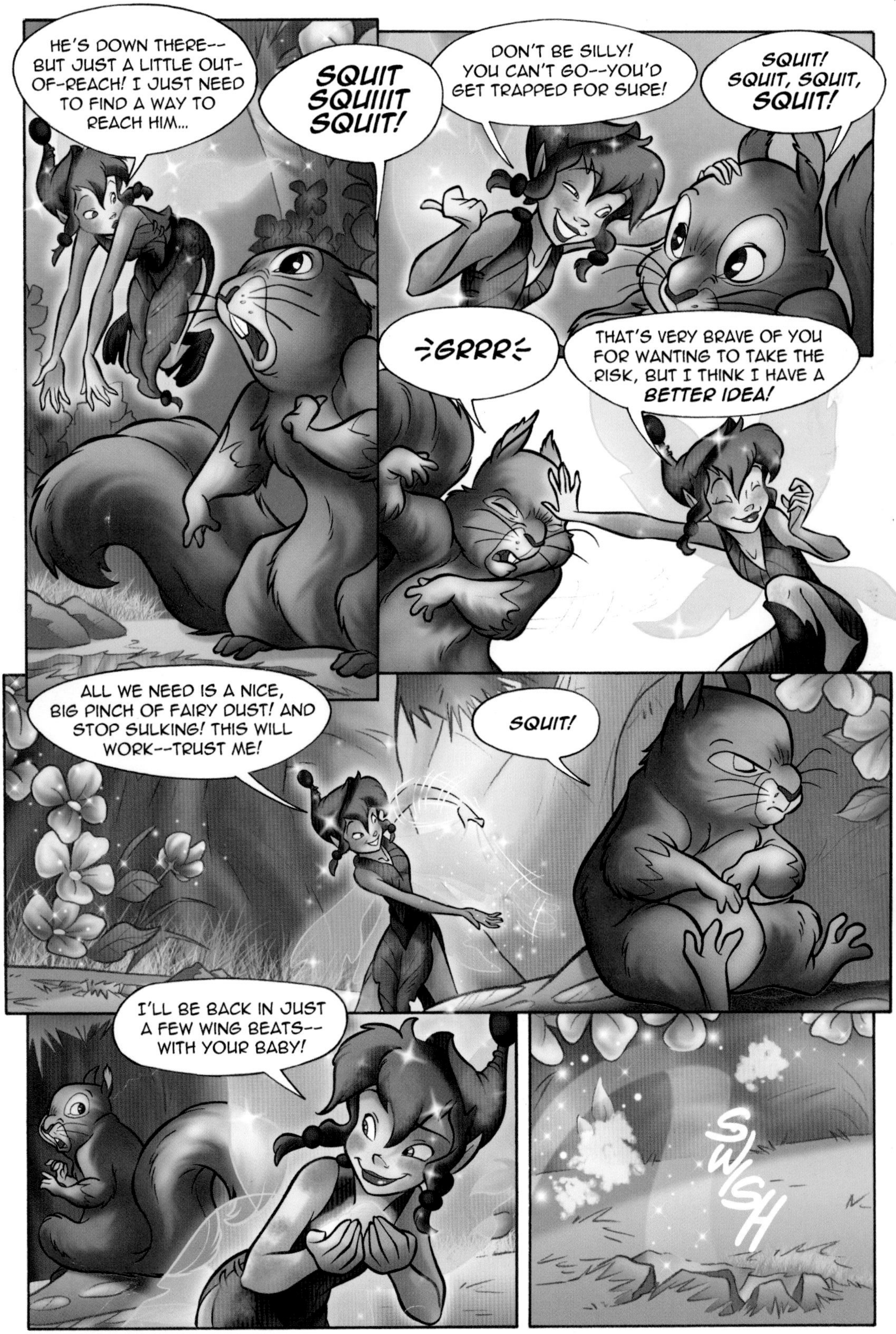
HE'S DOWN THERE--BUT JUST A LITTLE OUT-OF-REACH! I JUST NEED TO FIND A WAY TO REACH HIM...
SQUIT SQUIIIT SQUIT!
DON'T BE SILLY! YOU CAN'T GO--YOU'D GET TRAPPED FOR SURE!
SQUIT! SQUIT, SQUIT, SQUIT!
GRRR
THAT'S VERY BRAVE OF YOU FOR WANTING TO TAKE THE RISK, BUT I THINK I HAVE A BETTER IDEA!
ALL WE NEED IS A NICE, BIG PINCH OF FAIRY DUST! AND STOP SULKING! THIS WILL WORK--TRUST ME!
SQUIT!
I'LL BE BACK IN JUST A FEW WING BEATS--WITH YOUR BABY!
SWISH

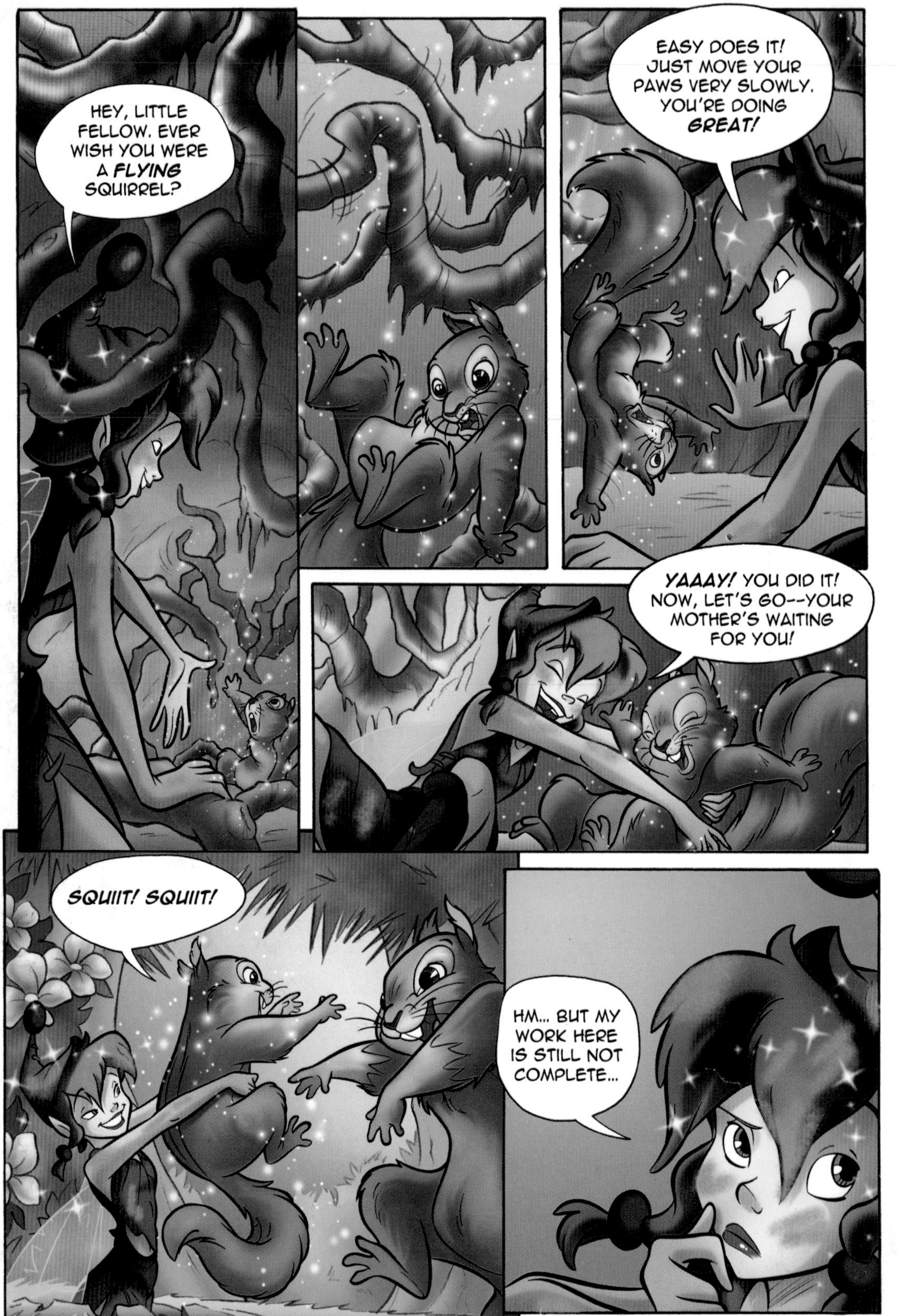
HEY, LITTLE FELLOW. EVER WISH YOU WERE A FLYING SQUIRREL?
EASY DOES IT! JUST MOVE YOUR PAWS VERY SLOWLY. YOU'RE DOING GREAT!
YAAAY! YOU DID IT! NOW, LET'S GO--YOUR MOTHER'S WAITING FOR YOU!
SQUIIT! SQUIIT!
HM... BUT MY WORK HERE IS STILL NOT COMPLETE...

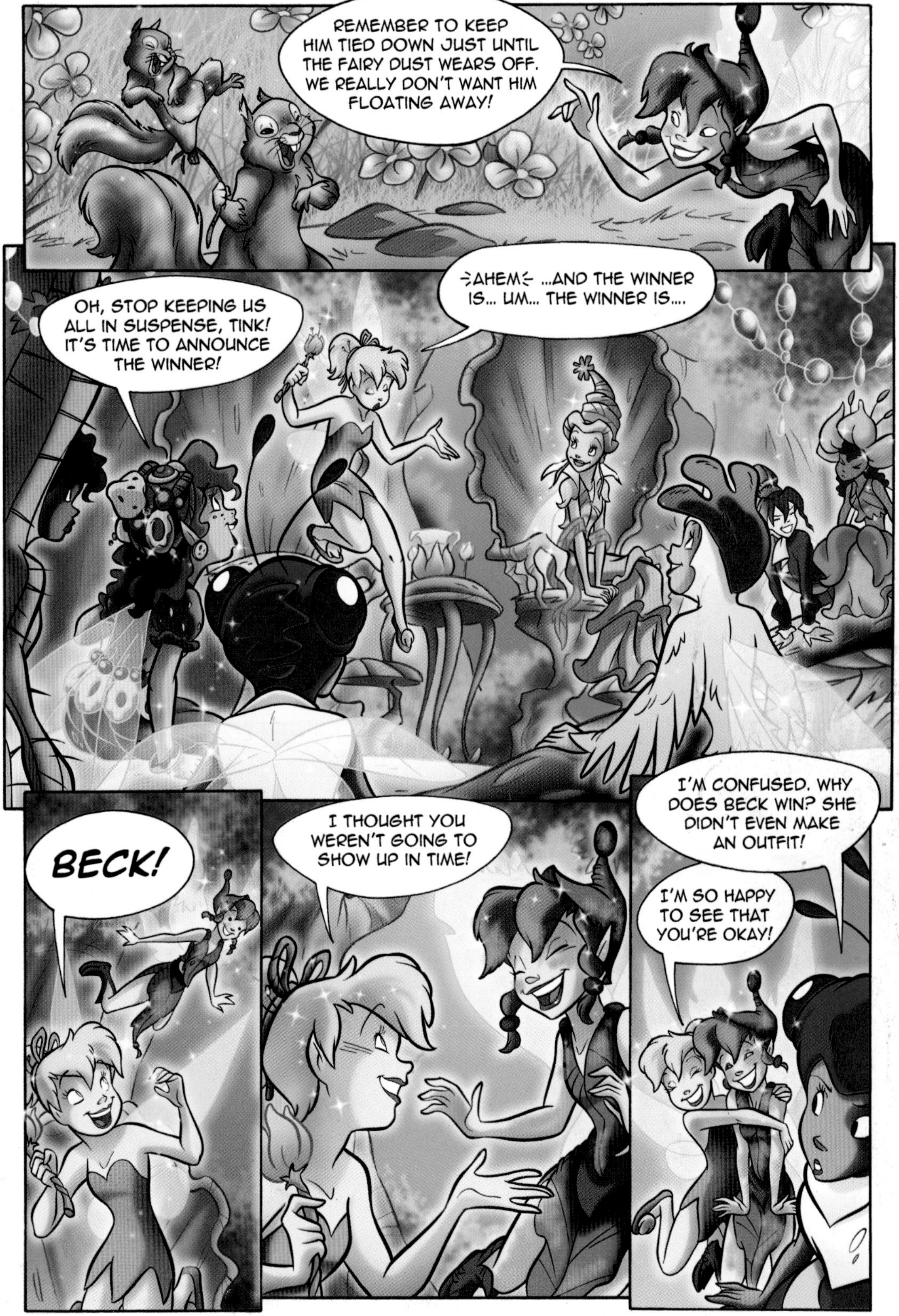
REMEMBER TO KEEP HIM TIED DOWN JUST UNTIL THE FAIRY DUST WEARS OFF. WE REALLY DON'T WANT HIM FLOATING AWAY!
OH, STOP KEEPING US ALL IN SUSPENSE, TINK! IT'S TIME TO ANNOUNCE THE WINNER!
AHEM ...AND THE WINNER IS... UM... THE WINNER IS....
BECK!
I THOUGHT YOU WEREN'T GOING TO SHOW UP IN TIME!
I'M CONFUSED. WHY DOES BECK WIN? SHE DIDN'T EVEN MAKE AN OUTFIT!
I'M SO HAPPY TO SEE THAT YOU'RE OKAY!

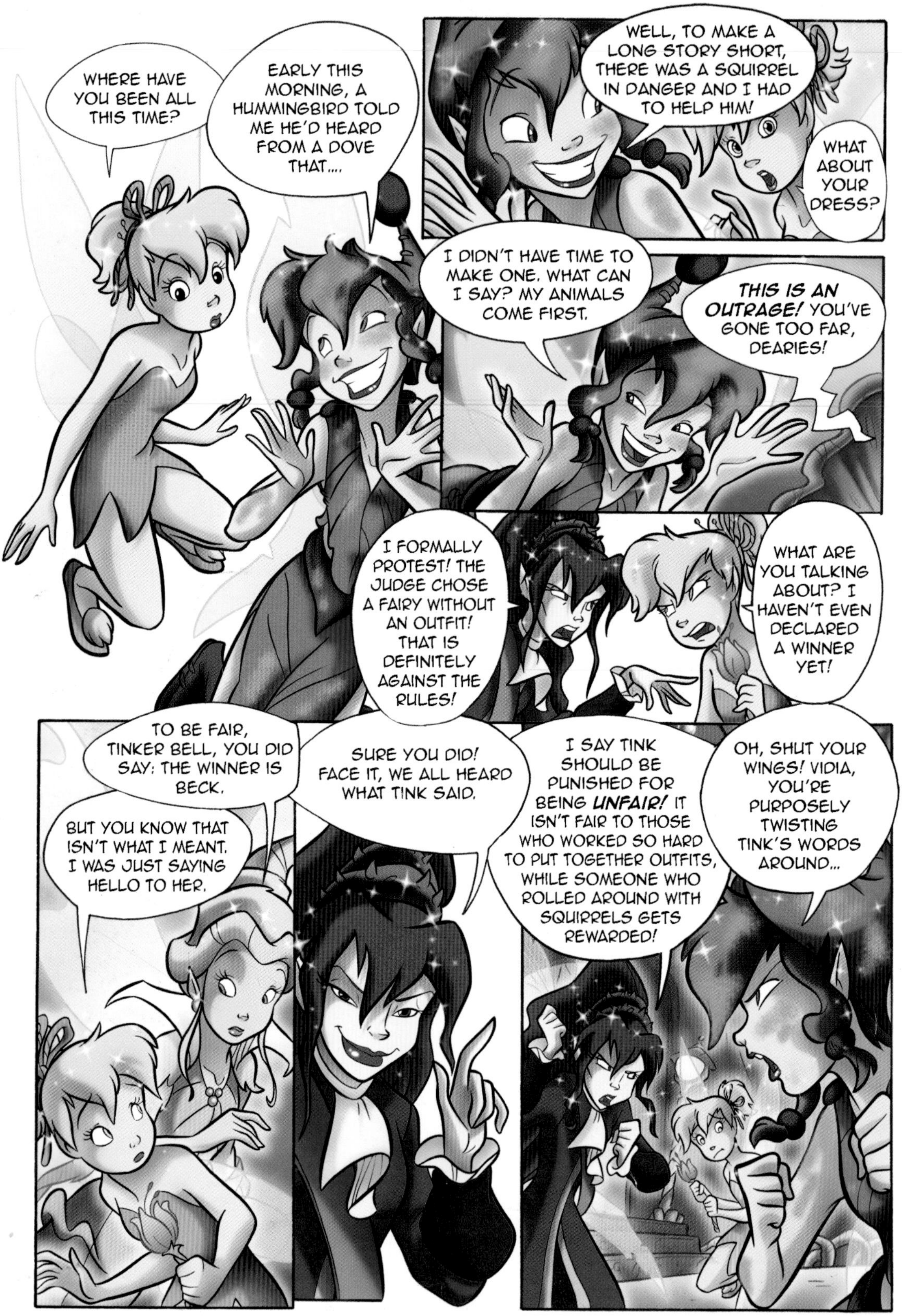
WHERE HAVE YOU BEEN ALL THIS TIME?
EARLY THIS MORNING, A HUMMINGBIRD TOLD ME HE'D HEARD FROM A DOVE THAT....
WELL, TO MAKE A LONG STORY SHORT, THERE WAS A SQUIRREL IN DANGER AND I HAD TO HELP HIM!
WHAT ABOUT YOUR DRESS?
I DIDN'T HAVE TIME TO MAKE ONE. WHAT CAN I SAY? MY ANIMALS COME FIRST.
THIS IS AN OUTRAGE! YOU'VE GONE TOO FAR, DEARIES!
I FORMALLY PROTEST! THE JUDGE CHOSE A FAIRY WITHOUT AN OUTFIT! THAT IS DEFINITELY AGAINST THE RULES!
WHAT ARE YOU TALKING ABOUT? I HAVEN'T EVEN DECLARED A WINNER YET!
TO BE FAIR, TINKER BELL, YOU DID SAY: THE WINNER IS BECK.
BUT YOU KNOW THAT ISN'T WHAT I MEANT. I WAS JUST SAYING HELLO TO HER.
SURE YOU DID! FACE IT, WE ALL HEARD WHAT TINK SAID.
I SAY TINK SHOULD BE PUNISHED FOR BEING UNFAIR! IT ISN'T FAIR TO THOSE WHO WORKED SO HARD TO PUT TOGETHER OUTFITS, WHILE SOMEONE WHO ROLLED AROUND WITH SQUIRRELS GETS REWARDED!
OH, SHUT YOUR WINGS! VIDIA, YOU'RE PURPOSELY TWISTING TINK'S WORDS AROUND...

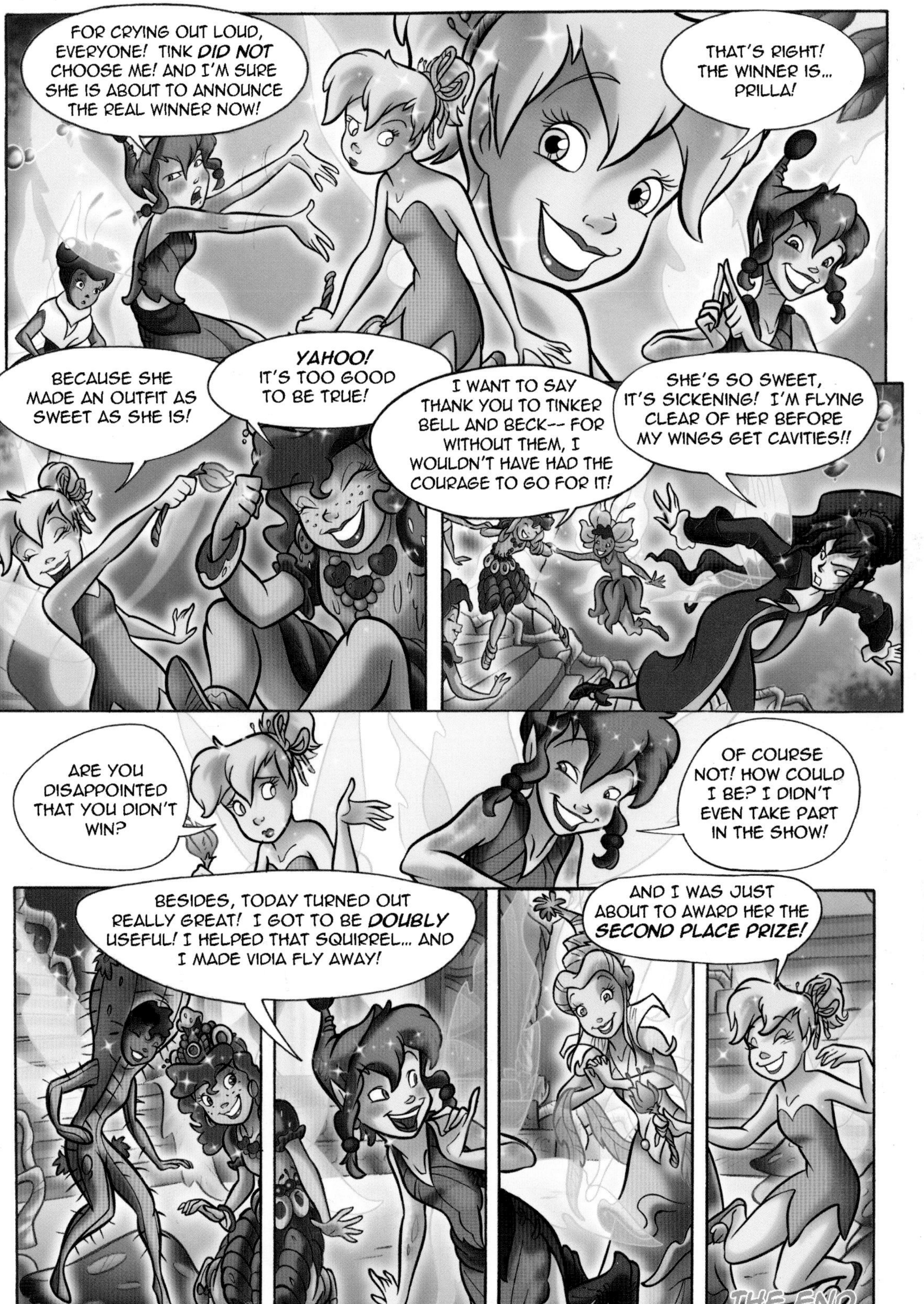
FOR CRYING OUT LOUD, EVERYONE! TINK DID NOT CHOOSE ME! AND I'M SURE SHE IS ABOUT TO ANNOUNCE THE REAL WINNER NOW!
THAT'S RIGHT! THE WINNER IS... PRILLA!
BECAUSE SHE MADE AN OUTFIT AS SWEET AS SHE IS!
YAHOO! IT'S TOO GOOD TO BE TRUE!
I WANT TO SAY THANK YOU TO TINKER BELL AND BECK-- FOR WITHOUT THEM, I WOULDN'T HAVE HAD THE COURAGE TO GO FOR IT!
SHE'S SO SWEET, IT'S SICKENING! I'M FLYING CLEAR OF HER BEFORE MY WINGS GET CAVITIES!!
ARE YOU DISAPPOINTED THAT YOU DIDN'T WIN?
OF COURSE NOT! HOW COULD I BE? I DIDN'T EVEN TAKE PART IN THE SHOW!
BESIDES, TODAY TURNED OUT REALLY GREAT! I GOT TO BE DOUBLY USEFUL! I HELPED THAT SQUIRREL... AND I MADE VIDIA FLY AWAY!
AND I WAS JUST ABOUT TO AWARD HER THE SECOND PLACE PRIZE!
THE END

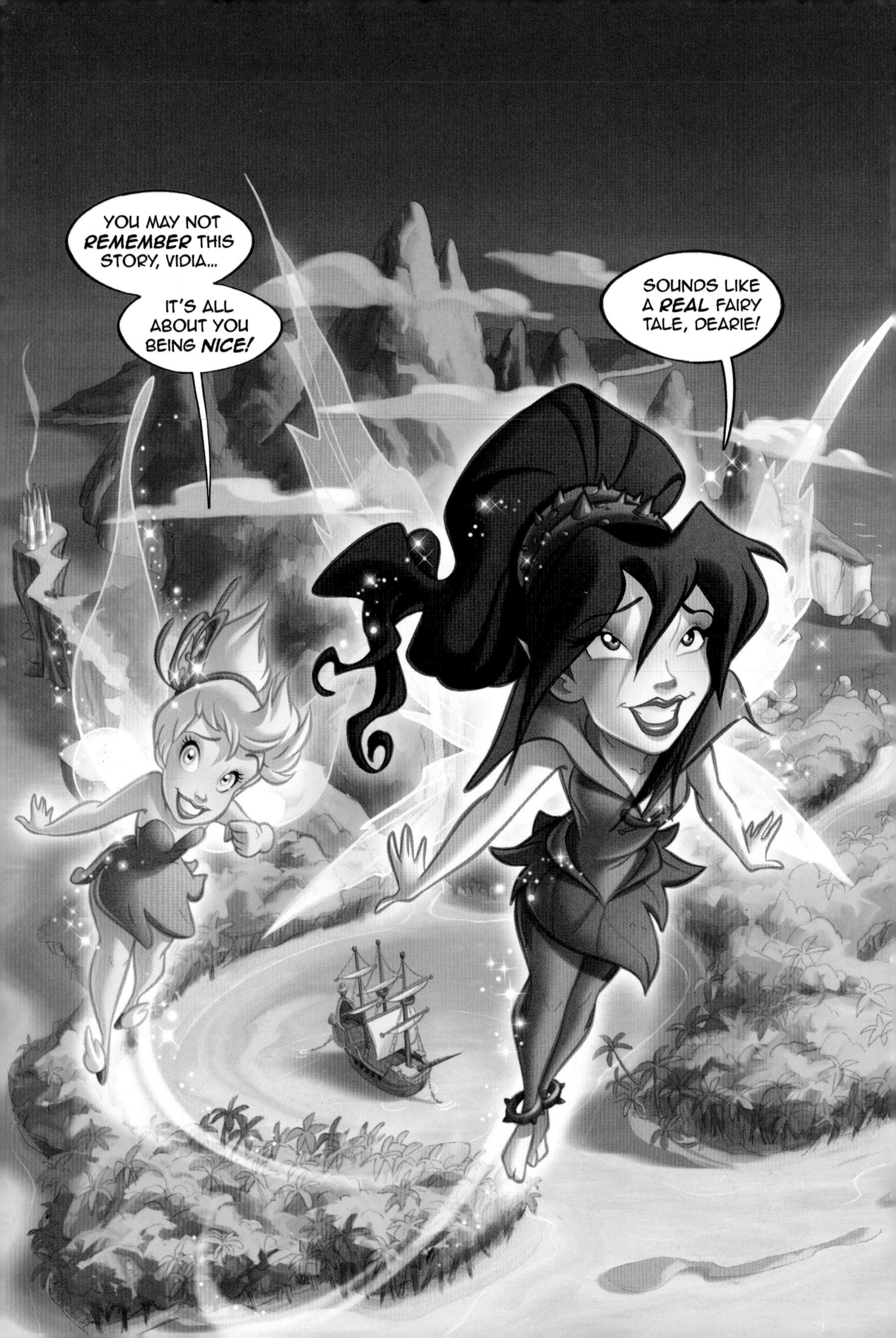
YOU MAY NOT REMEMBER THIS STORY, VIDIA...
IT'S ALL ABOUT YOU BEING NICE!
SOUNDS LIKE A REAL FAIRY TALE, DEARIE!

Vidia Turns Nice!

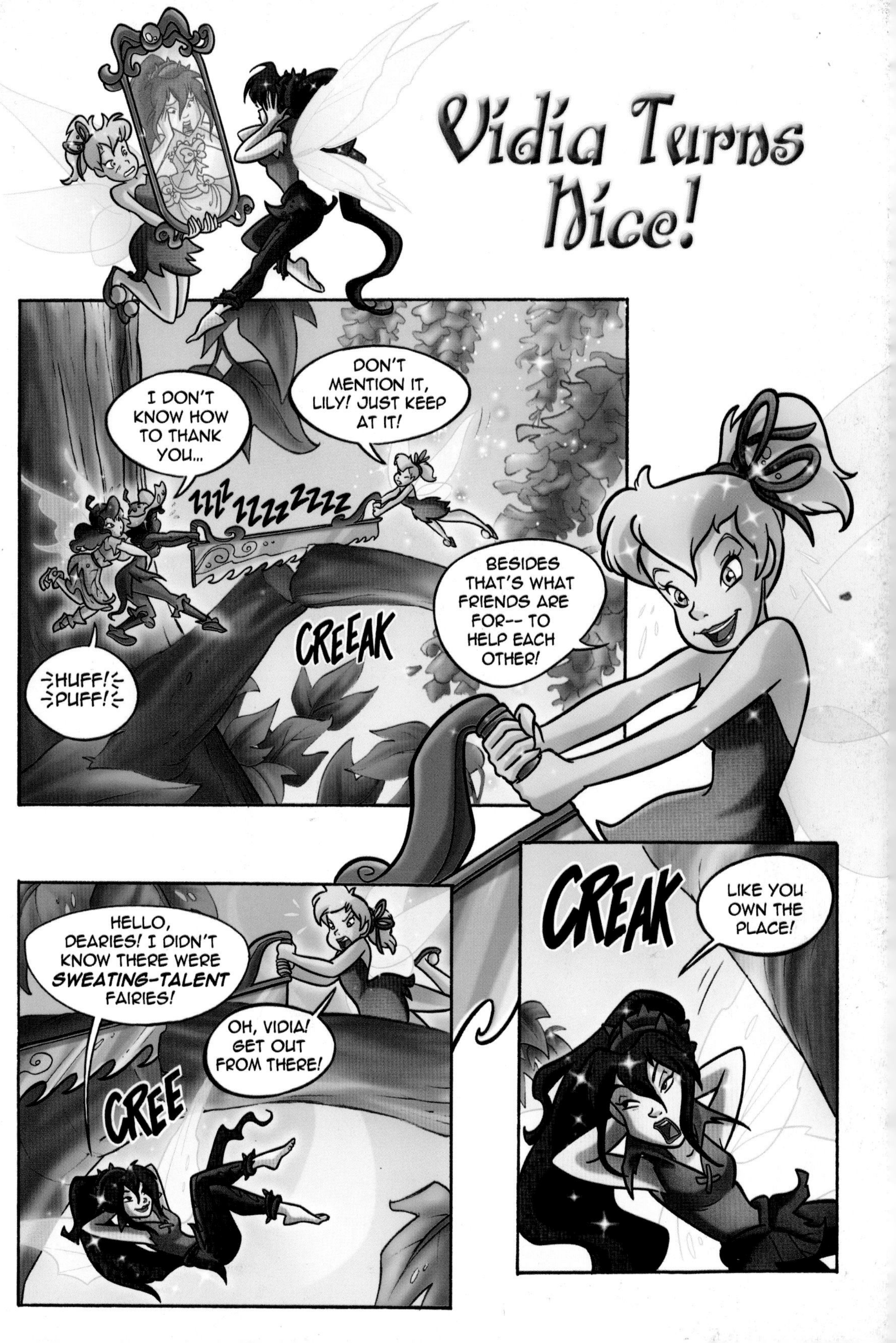
I DON'T KNOW HOW TO THANK YOU...
ZZZZ ZZZZZZZZ
DON'T MENTION IT, LILY! JUST KEEP AT IT!
HUFF! PUFF!
CREEAK
BESIDES THAT'S WHAT FRIENDS ARE FOR-- TO HELP EACH OTHER!
HELLO, DEARIES! I DIDN'T KNOW THERE WERE *SWEATING-TALENT* FAIRIES!
OH, VIDIA! GET OUT FROM THERE!
CREE
CREAK
LIKE YOU OWN THE PLACE!

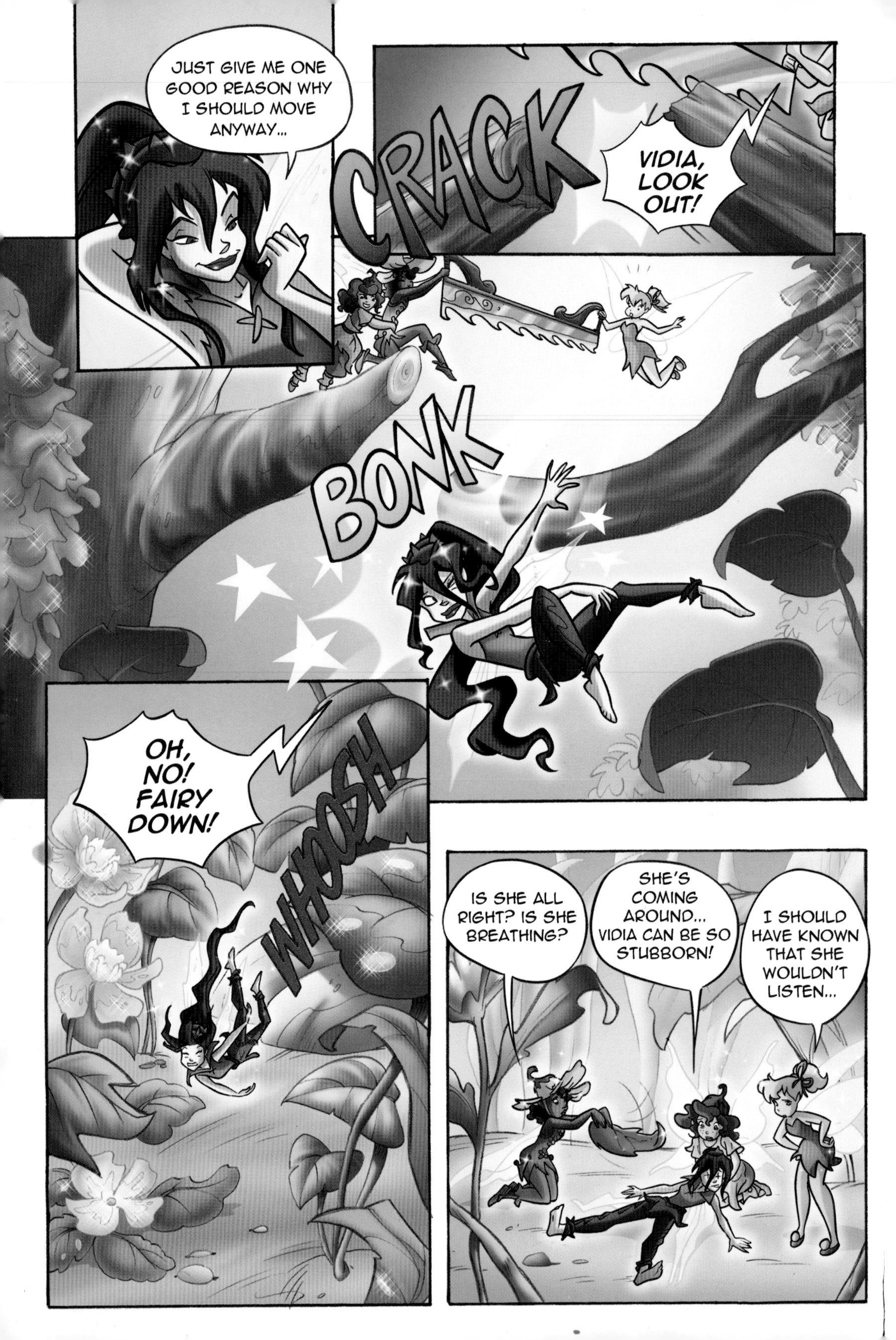

JUST GIVE ME ONE GOOD REASON WHY I SHOULD MOVE ANYWAY...
CRACK
VIDIA, LOOK OUT!
BONK
OH, NO! FAIRY DOWN!
WHOOSH
IS SHE ALL RIGHT? IS SHE BREATHING?
SHE'S COMING AROUND... VIDIA CAN BE SO STUBBORN!
I SHOULD HAVE KNOWN THAT SHE WOULDN'T LISTEN...

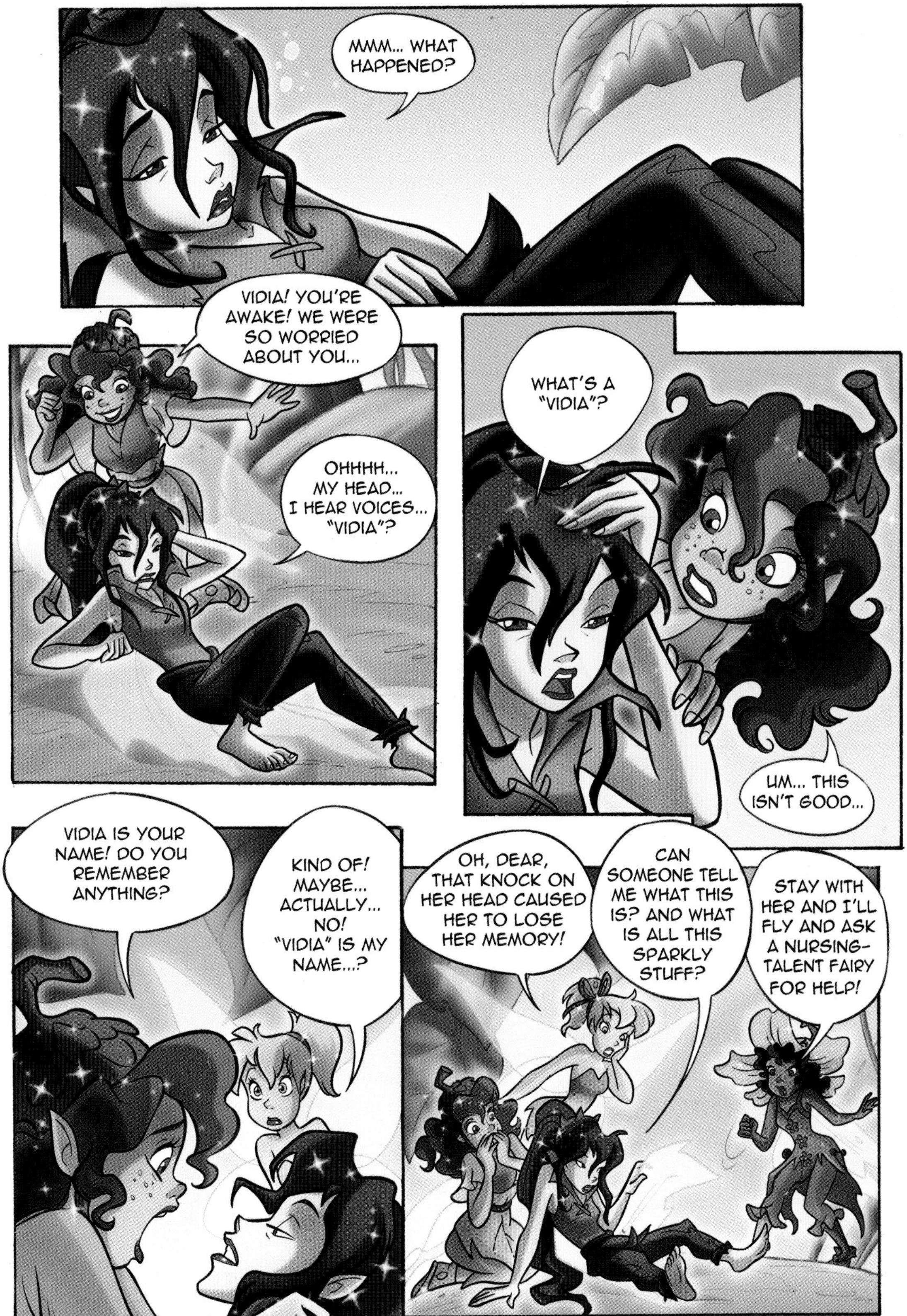
MMM... WHAT HAPPENED?
VIDIA! YOU'RE AWAKE! WE WERE SO WORRIED ABOUT YOU...
OHHHH... MY HEAD... I HEAR VOICES... "VIDIA"?
WHAT'S A "VIDIA"?
UM... THIS ISN'T GOOD...
VIDIA IS YOUR NAME! DO YOU REMEMBER ANYTHING?
KIND OF! MAYBE... ACTUALLY... NO! "VIDIA" IS MY NAME...?
OH, DEAR, THAT KNOCK ON HER HEAD CAUSED HER TO LOSE HER MEMORY!
CAN SOMEONE TELL ME WHAT THIS IS? AND WHAT IS ALL THIS SPARKLY STUFF?
STAY WITH HER AND I'LL FLY AND ASK A NURSING-TALENT FAIRY FOR HELP!

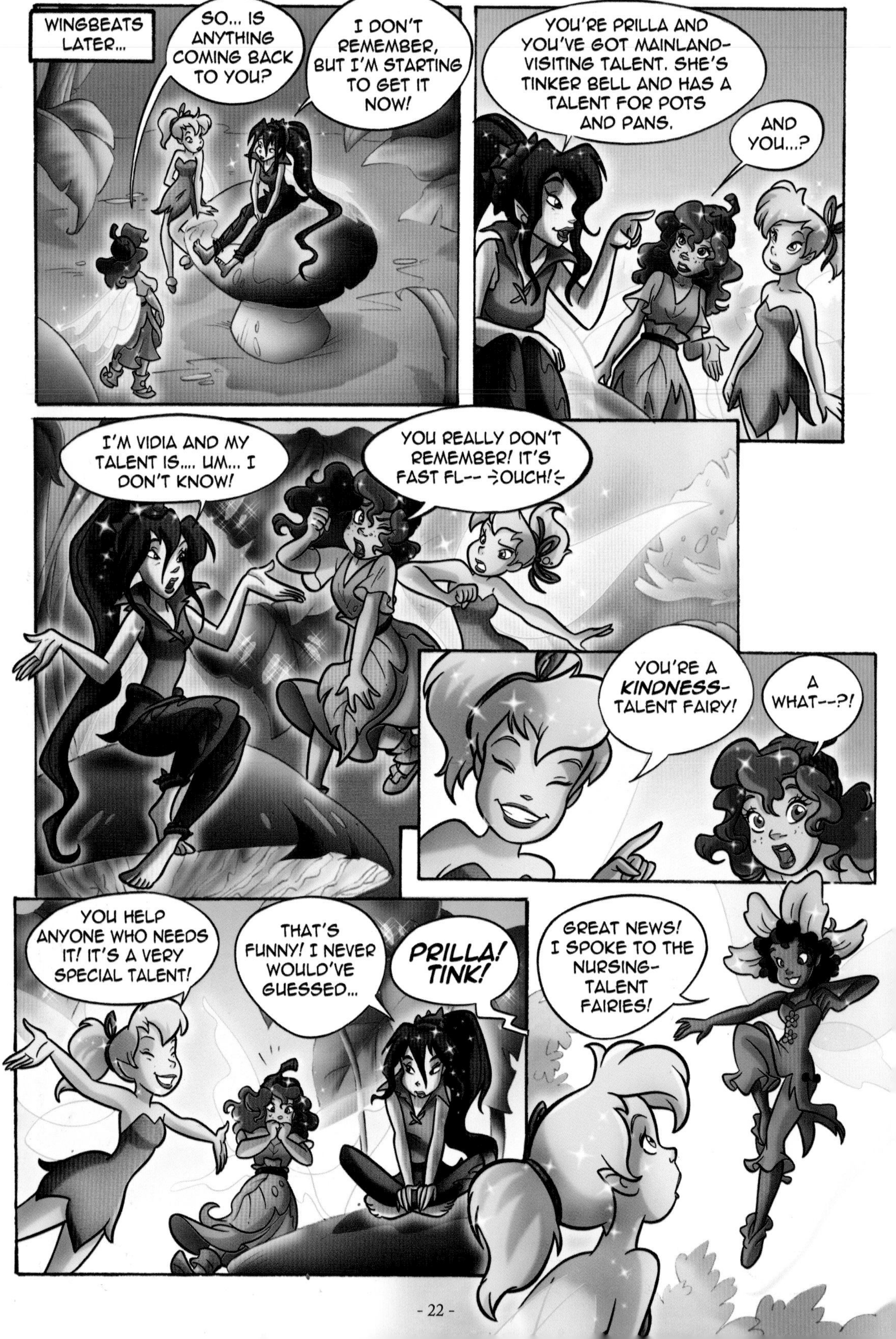
WINGBEATS LATER...
SO... IS ANYTHING COMING BACK TO YOU?
I DON'T REMEMBER, BUT I'M STARTING TO GET IT NOW!
YOU'RE PRILLA AND YOU'VE GOT MAINLAND-VISITING TALENT. SHE'S TINKER BELL AND HAS A TALENT FOR POTS AND PANS.
AND YOU...?
I'M VIDIA AND MY TALENT IS.... UM... I DON'T KNOW!
YOU REALLY DON'T REMEMBER! IT'S FAST FL-- OUCH!
YOU'RE A KINDNESS-TALENT FAIRY!
A WHAT--?!
YOU HELP ANYONE WHO NEEDS IT! IT'S A VERY SPECIAL TALENT!
THAT'S FUNNY! I NEVER WOULD'VE GUESSED...
PRILLA! TINK!
GREAT NEWS! I SPOKE TO THE NURSING-TALENT FAIRIES!

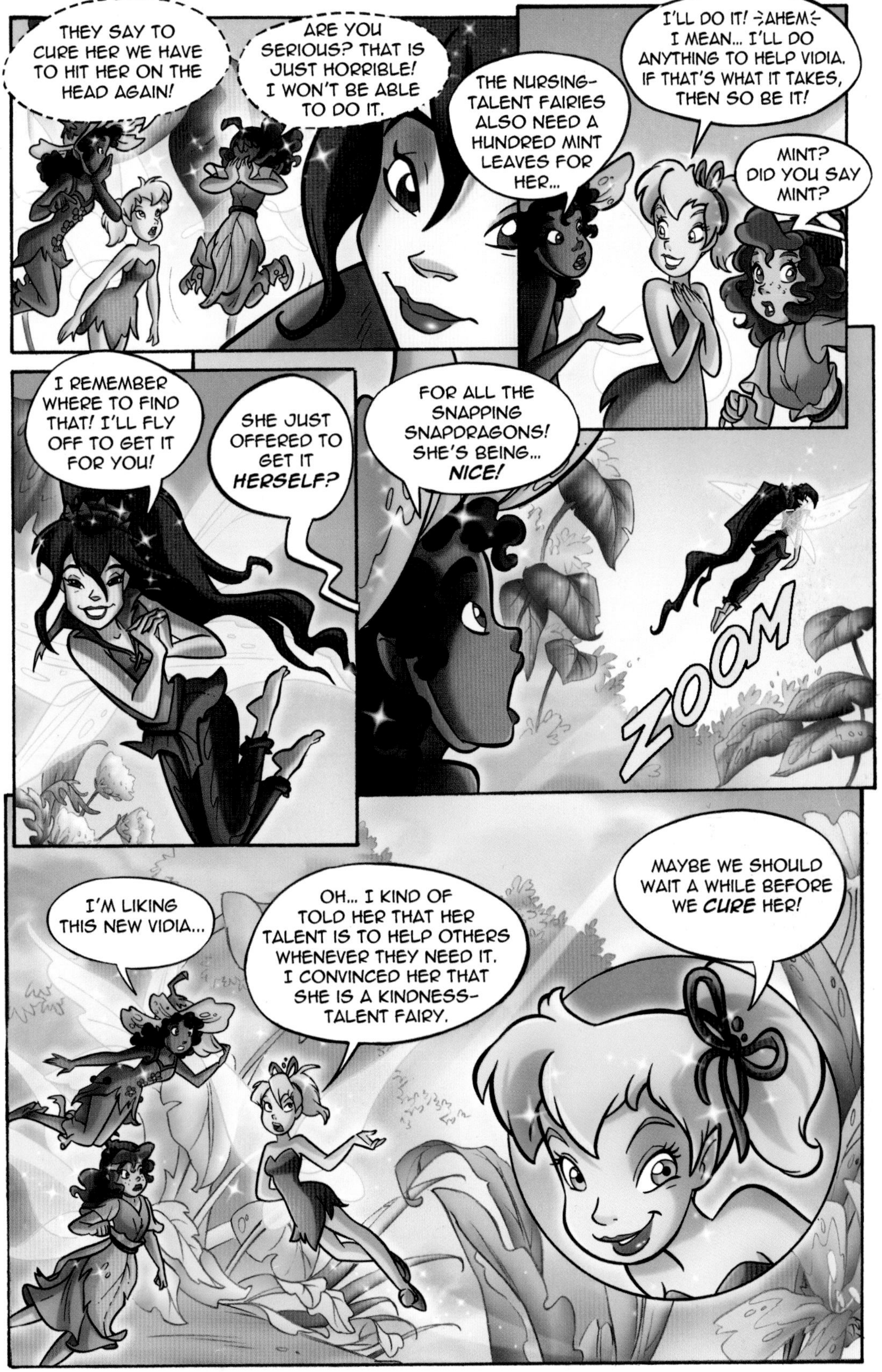
THEY SAY TO CURE HER WE HAVE TO HIT HER ON THE HEAD AGAIN!
ARE YOU SERIOUS? THAT IS JUST HORRIBLE! I WON'T BE ABLE TO DO IT.
THE NURSING-TALENT FAIRIES ALSO NEED A HUNDRED MINT LEAVES FOR HER...
I'LL DO IT! AHEM I MEAN... I'LL DO ANYTHING TO HELP VIDIA. IF THAT'S WHAT IT TAKES, THEN SO BE IT!
MINT? DID YOU SAY MINT?
I REMEMBER WHERE TO FIND THAT! I'LL FLY OFF TO GET IT FOR YOU!
SHE JUST OFFERED TO GET IT *HERSELF?*
FOR ALL THE SNAPPING SNAPDRAGONS! SHE'S BEING... *NICE!*
ZOOM
I'M LIKING THIS NEW VIDIA...
OH... I KIND OF TOLD HER THAT HER TALENT IS TO HELP OTHERS WHENEVER THEY NEED IT. I CONVINCED HER THAT SHE IS A KINDNESS-TALENT FAIRY.
MAYBE WE SHOULD WAIT A WHILE BEFORE WE *CURE* HER!

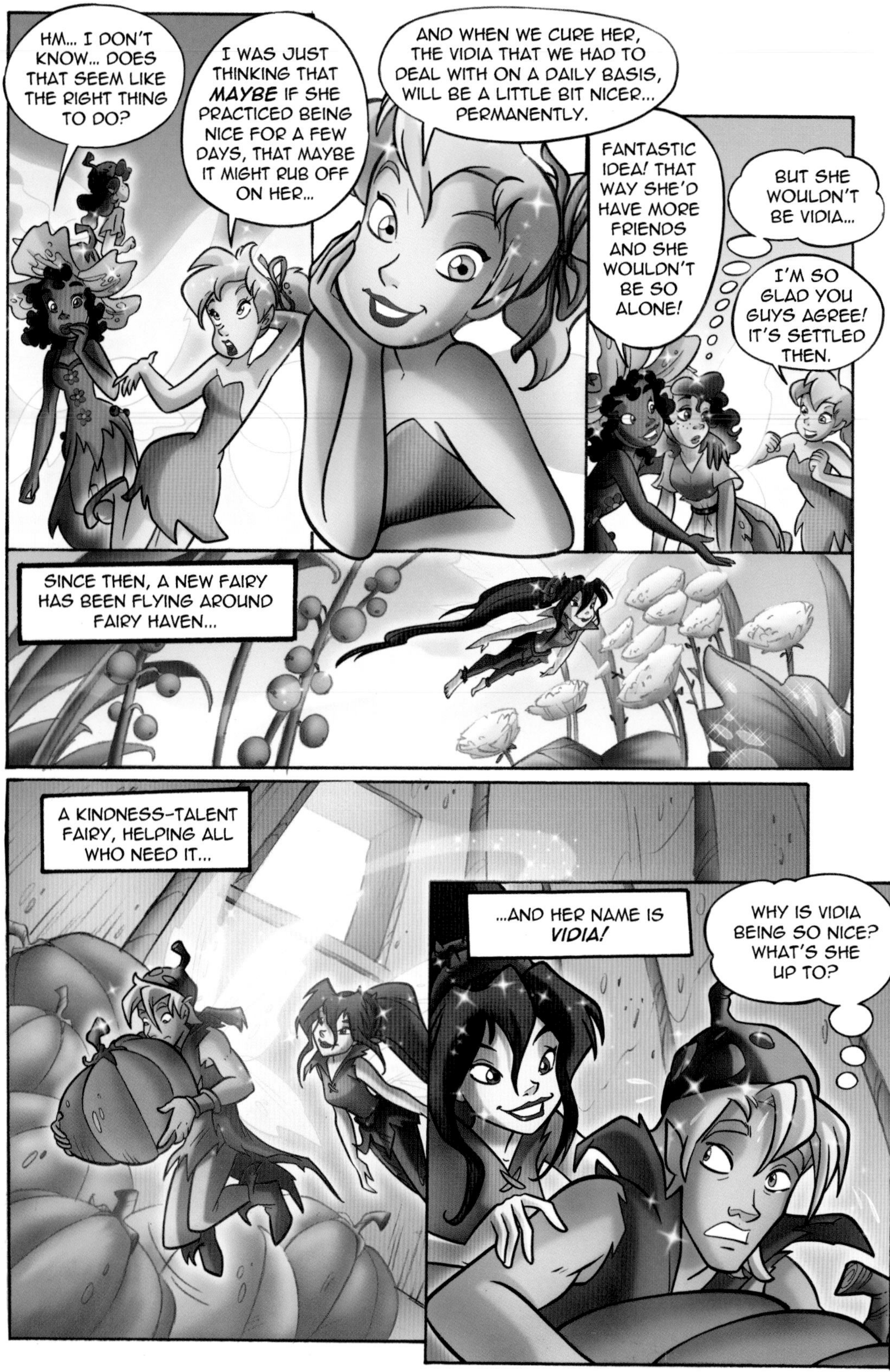
HM... I DON'T KNOW... DOES THAT SEEM LIKE THE RIGHT THING TO DO?
I WAS JUST THINKING THAT *MAYBE* IF SHE PRACTICED BEING NICE FOR A FEW DAYS, THAT MAYBE IT MIGHT RUB OFF ON HER...
AND WHEN WE CURE HER, THE VIDIA THAT WE HAD TO DEAL WITH ON A DAILY BASIS, WILL BE A LITTLE BIT NICER... PERMANENTLY.
FANTASTIC IDEA! THAT WAY SHE'D HAVE MORE FRIENDS AND SHE WOULDN'T BE SO ALONE!
BUT SHE WOULDN'T BE VIDIA...
I'M SO GLAD YOU GUYS AGREE! IT'S SETTLED THEN.
SINCE THEN, A NEW FAIRY HAS BEEN FLYING AROUND FAIRY HAVEN...
A KINDNESS-TALENT FAIRY, HELPING ALL WHO NEED IT...
...AND HER NAME IS *VIDIA!*
WHY IS VIDIA BEING SO NICE? WHAT'S SHE UP TO?

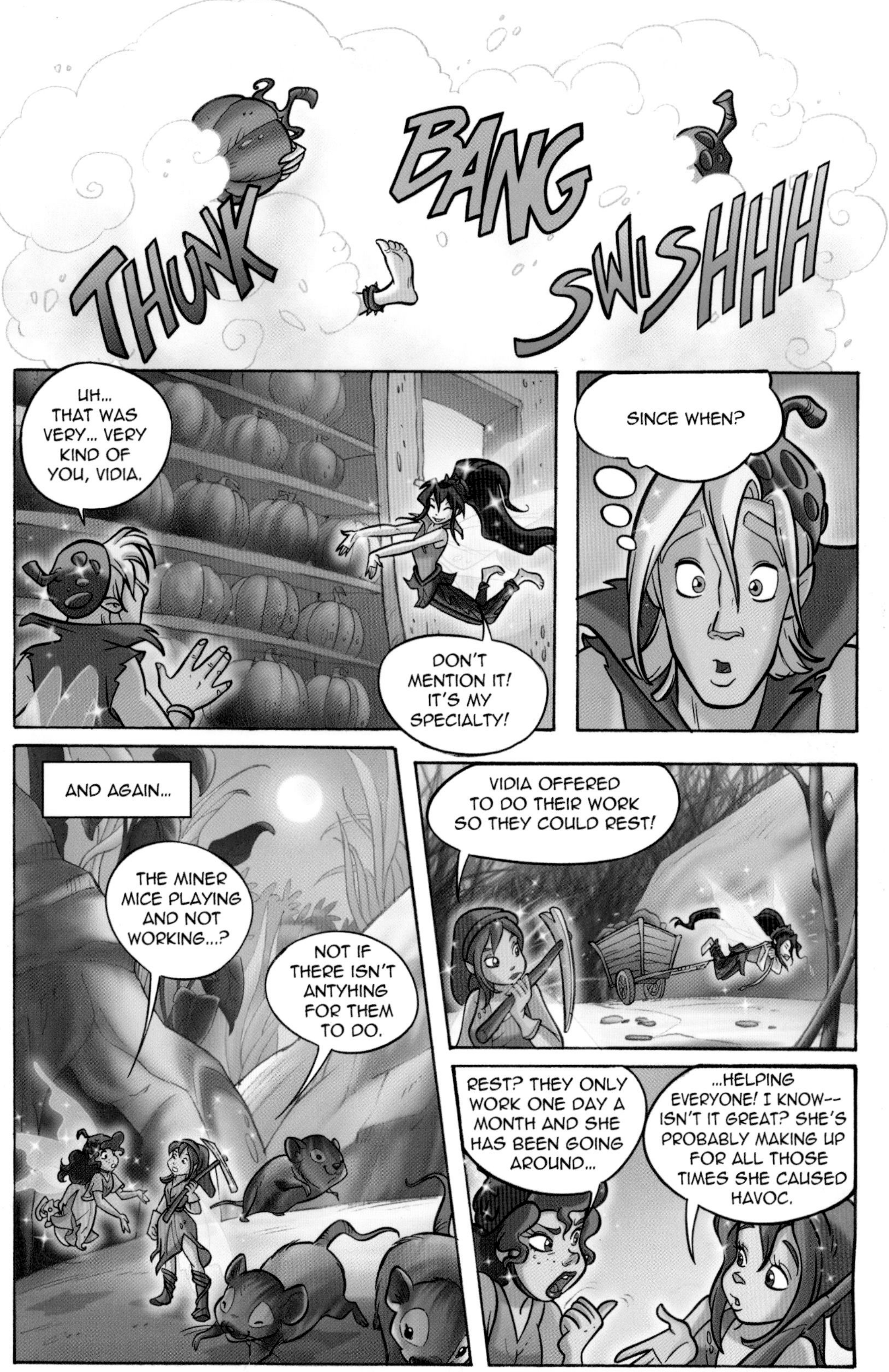
THUNK
BANG
SWISHHH
UH... THAT WAS VERY... VERY KIND OF YOU, VIDIA.
DON'T MENTION IT! IT'S MY SPECIALTY!
SINCE WHEN?
AND AGAIN...
THE MINER MICE PLAYING AND NOT WORKING...?
NOT IF THERE ISN'T ANTYHING FOR THEM TO DO.
VIDIA OFFERED TO DO THEIR WORK SO THEY COULD REST!
REST? THEY ONLY WORK ONE DAY A MONTH AND SHE HAS BEEN GOING AROUND...
...HELPING EVERYONE! I KNOW-- ISN'T IT GREAT? SHE'S PROBABLY MAKING UP FOR ALL THOSE TIMES SHE CAUSED HAVOC.

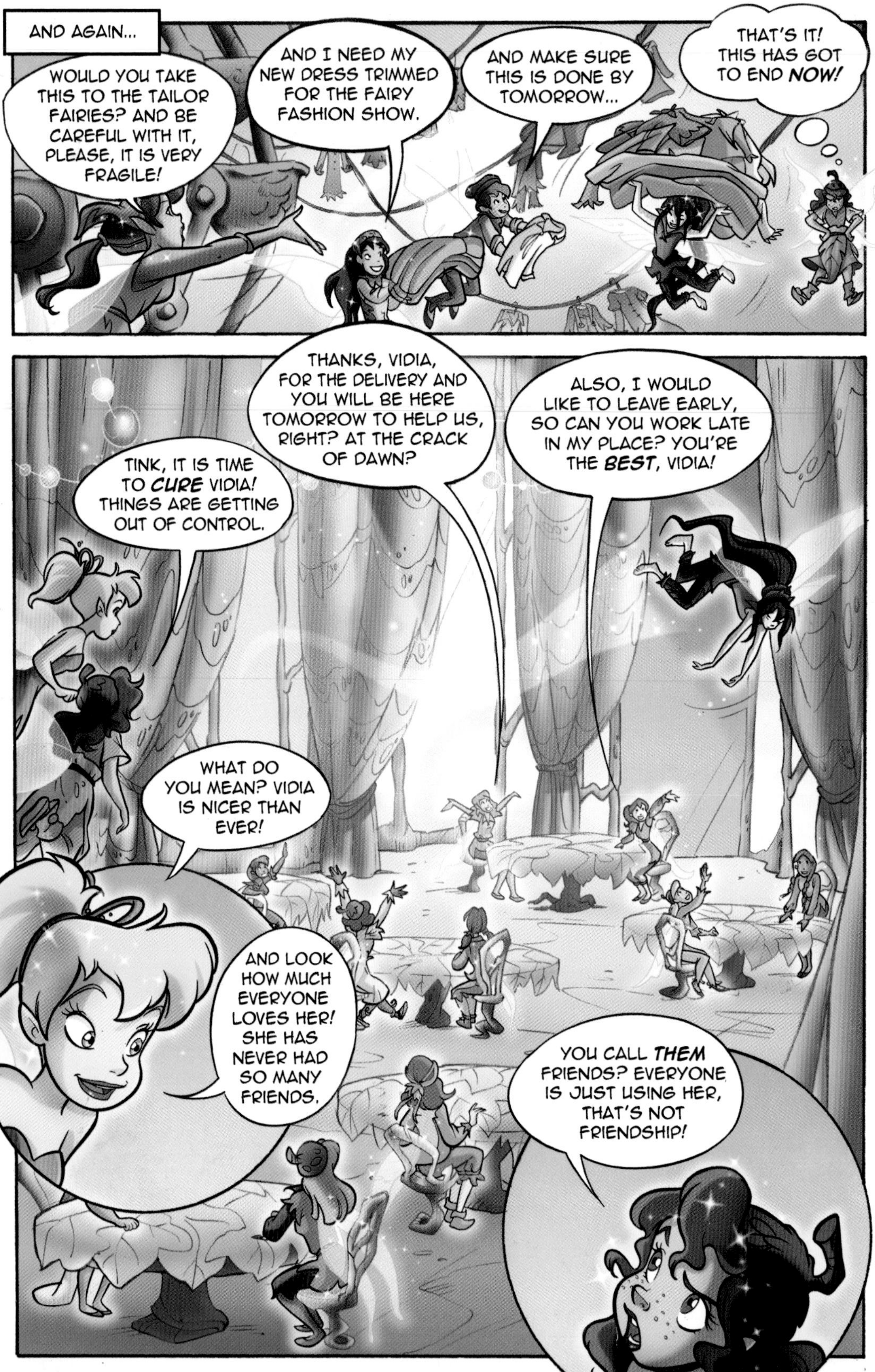
AND AGAIN...
WOULD YOU TAKE THIS TO THE TAILOR FAIRIES? AND BE CAREFUL WITH IT, PLEASE, IT IS VERY FRAGILE!
AND I NEED MY NEW DRESS TRIMMED FOR THE FAIRY FASHION SHOW.
AND MAKE SURE THIS IS DONE BY TOMORROW...
THAT'S IT! THIS HAS GOT TO END NOW!
THANKS, VIDIA, FOR THE DELIVERY AND YOU WILL BE HERE TOMORROW TO HELP US, RIGHT? AT THE CRACK OF DAWN?
ALSO, I WOULD LIKE TO LEAVE EARLY, SO CAN YOU WORK LATE IN MY PLACE? YOU'RE THE BEST, VIDIA!
TINK, IT IS TIME TO CURE VIDIA! THINGS ARE GETTING OUT OF CONTROL.
WHAT DO YOU MEAN? VIDIA IS NICER THAN EVER!
AND LOOK HOW MUCH EVERYONE LOVES HER! SHE HAS NEVER HAD SO MANY FRIENDS.
YOU CALL THEM FRIENDS? EVERYONE IS JUST USING HER, THAT'S NOT FRIENDSHIP!

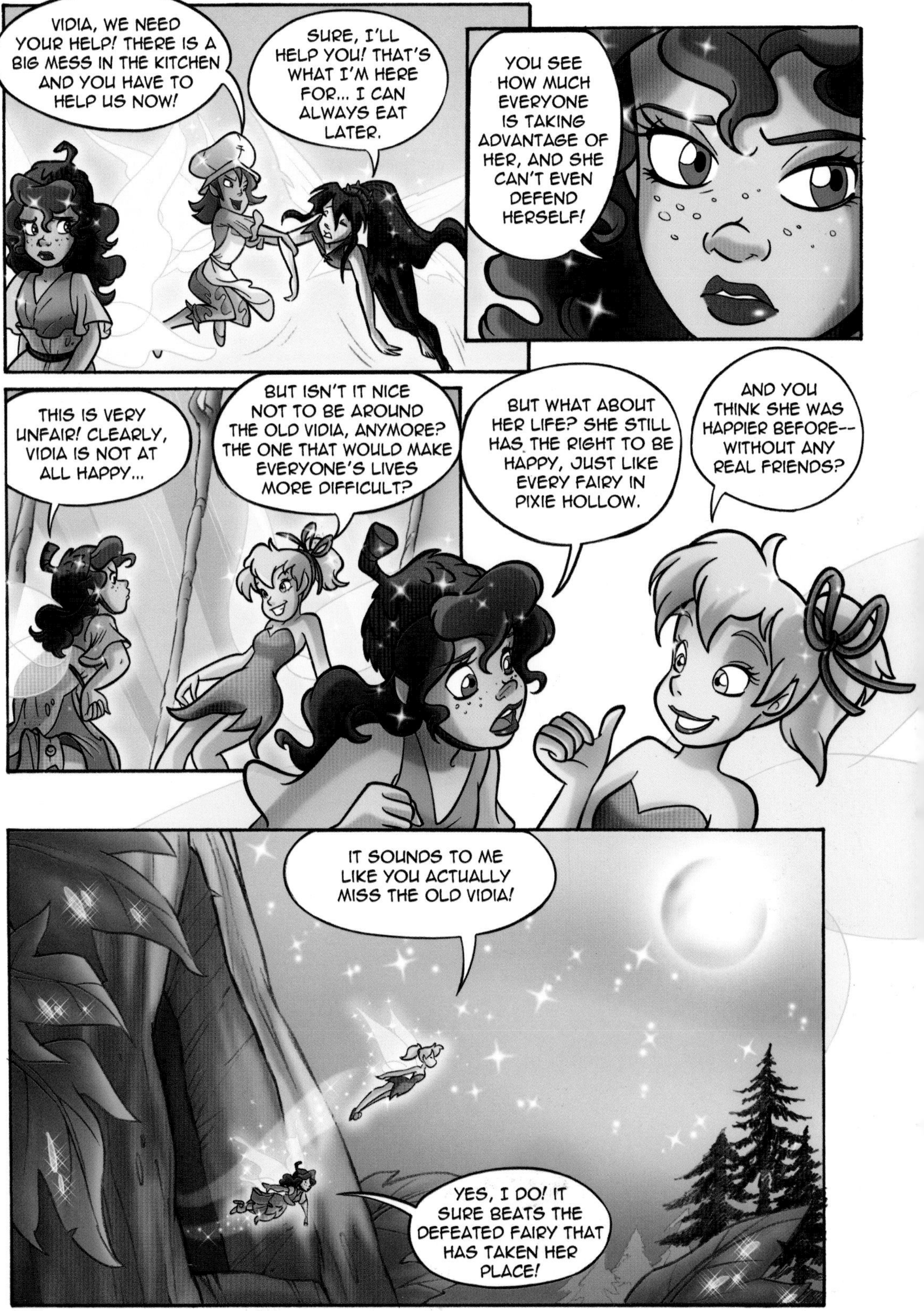
VIDIA, WE NEED YOUR HELP! THERE IS A BIG MESS IN THE KITCHEN AND YOU HAVE TO HELP US NOW!
SURE, I'LL HELP YOU! THAT'S WHAT I'M HERE FOR... I CAN ALWAYS EAT LATER.
YOU SEE HOW MUCH EVERYONE IS TAKING ADVANTAGE OF HER, AND SHE CAN'T EVEN DEFEND HERSELF!
THIS IS VERY UNFAIR! CLEARLY, VIDIA IS NOT AT ALL HAPPY...
BUT ISN'T IT NICE NOT TO BE AROUND THE OLD VIDIA, ANYMORE? THE ONE THAT WOULD MAKE EVERYONE'S LIVES MORE DIFFICULT?
BUT WHAT ABOUT HER LIFE? SHE STILL HAS THE RIGHT TO BE HAPPY, JUST LIKE EVERY FAIRY IN PIXIE HOLLOW.
AND YOU THINK SHE WAS HAPPIER BEFORE-- WITHOUT ANY REAL FRIENDS?
IT SOUNDS TO ME LIKE YOU ACTUALLY MISS THE OLD VIDIA!
YES, I DO! IT SURE BEATS THE DEFEATED FAIRY THAT HAS TAKEN HER PLACE!

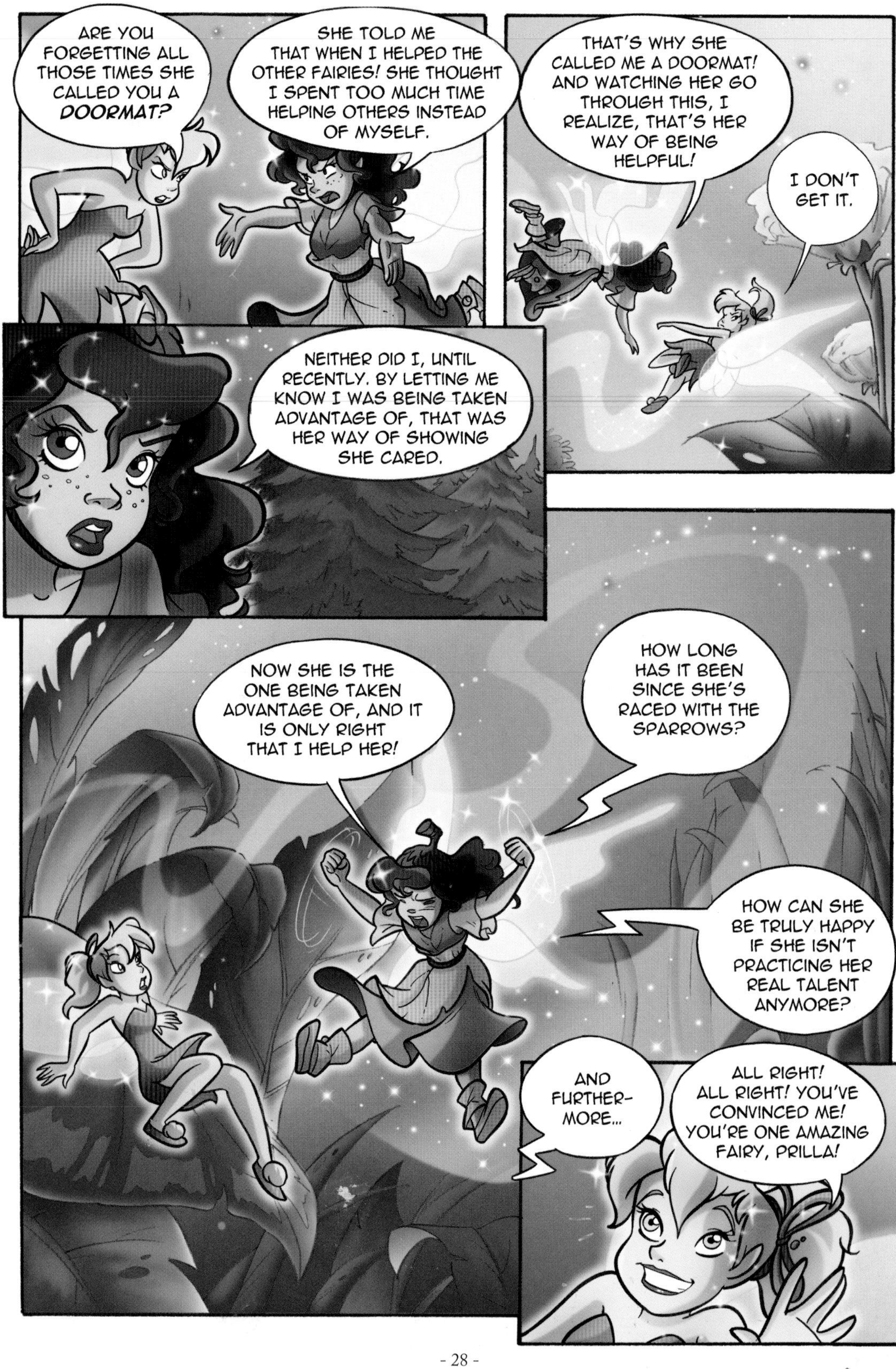
ARE YOU FORGETTING ALL THOSE TIMES SHE CALLED YOU A *DOORMAT?*
SHE TOLD ME THAT WHEN I HELPED THE OTHER FAIRIES! SHE THOUGHT I SPENT TOO MUCH TIME HELPING OTHERS INSTEAD OF MYSELF.
THAT'S WHY SHE CALLED ME A DOORMAT! AND WATCHING HER GO THROUGH THIS, I REALIZE, THAT'S HER WAY OF BEING HELPFUL!
I DON'T GET IT.
NEITHER DID I, UNTIL RECENTLY. BY LETTING ME KNOW I WAS BEING TAKEN ADVANTAGE OF, THAT WAS HER WAY OF SHOWING SHE CARED.
NOW SHE IS THE ONE BEING TAKEN ADVANTAGE OF, AND IT IS ONLY RIGHT THAT I HELP HER!
HOW LONG HAS IT BEEN SINCE SHE'S RACED WITH THE SPARROWS?
HOW CAN SHE BE TRULY HAPPY IF SHE ISN'T PRACTICING HER REAL TALENT ANYMORE?
AND FURTHER-MORE...
ALL RIGHT! ALL RIGHT! YOU'VE CONVINCED ME! YOU'RE ONE AMAZING FAIRY, PRILLA!

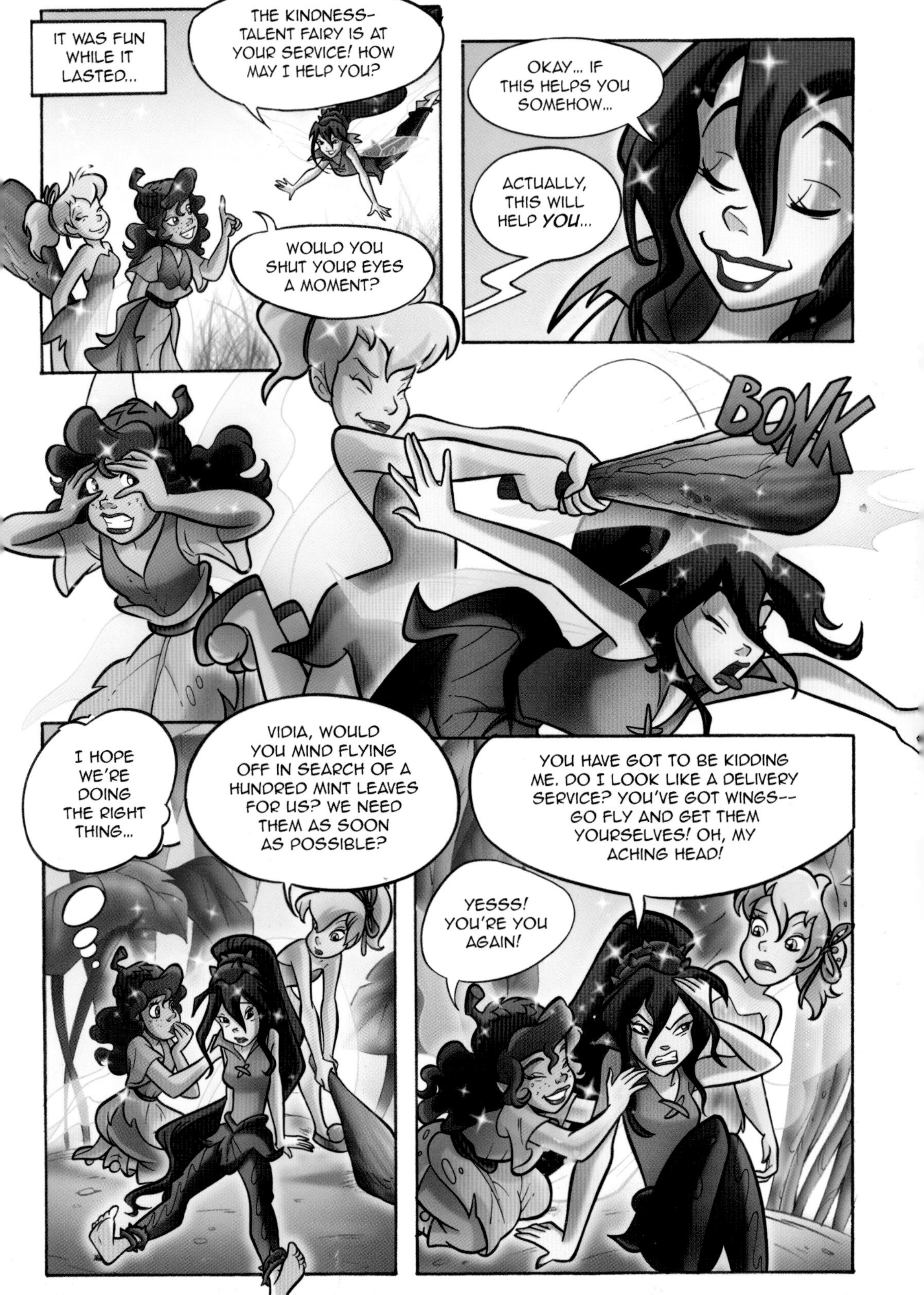

IT WAS FUN WHILE IT LASTED...
THE KINDNESS-TALENT FAIRY IS AT YOUR SERVICE! HOW MAY I HELP YOU?
WOULD YOU SHUT YOUR EYES A MOMENT?
OKAY... IF THIS HELPS YOU SOMEHOW...
ACTUALLY, THIS WILL HELP YOU...
BONK
I HOPE WE'RE DOING THE RIGHT THING...
VIDIA, WOULD YOU MIND FLYING OFF IN SEARCH OF A HUNDRED MINT LEAVES FOR US? WE NEED THEM AS SOON AS POSSIBLE?
YOU HAVE GOT TO BE KIDDING ME. DO I LOOK LIKE A DELIVERY SERVICE? YOU'VE GOT WINGS--GO FLY AND GET THEM YOURSELVES! OH, MY ACHING HEAD!
YESSS! YOU'RE YOU AGAIN!

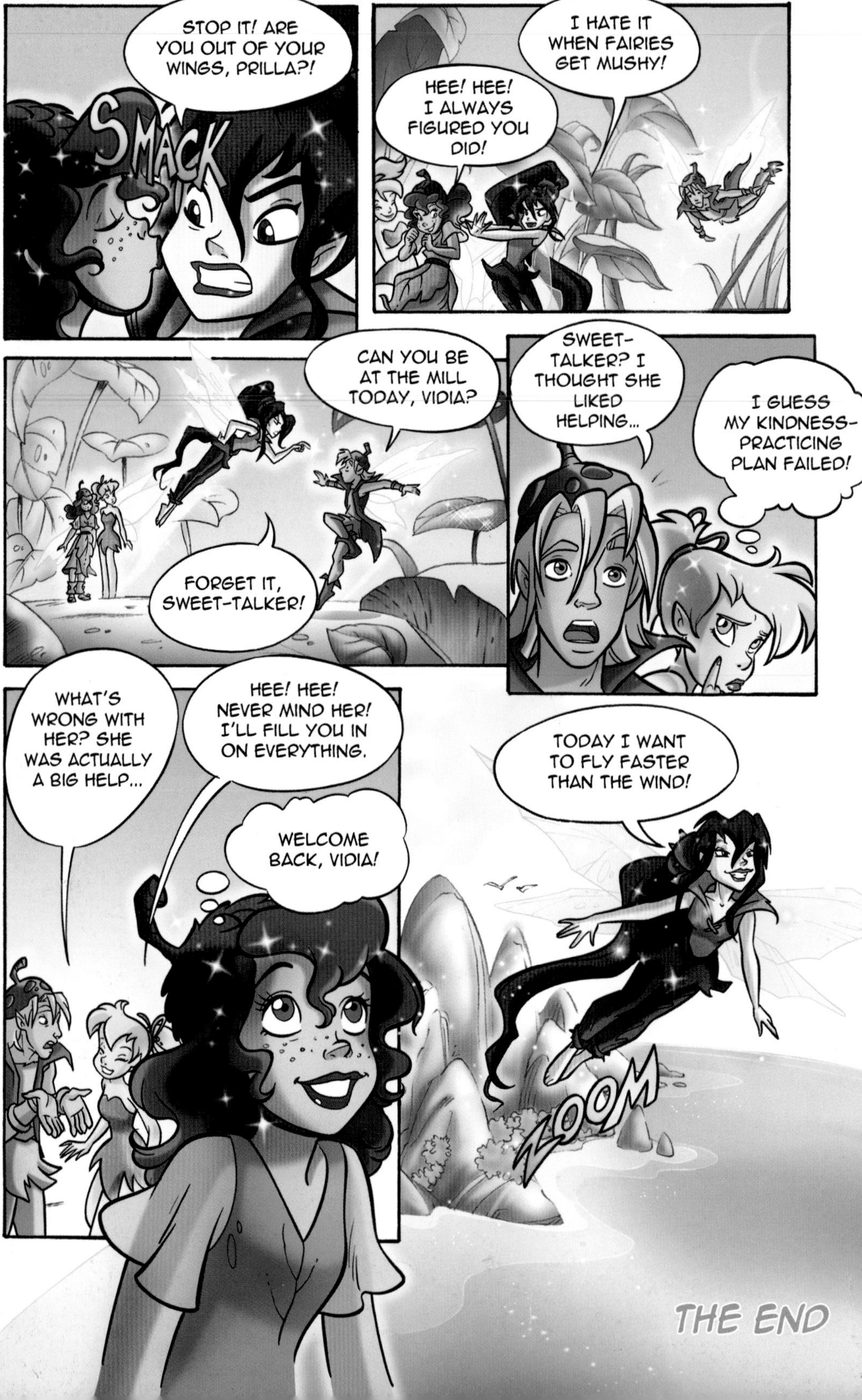
STOP IT! ARE YOU OUT OF YOUR WINGS, PRILLA?!
SMACK
I HATE IT WHEN FAIRIES GET MUSHY!
HEE! HEE! I ALWAYS FIGURED YOU DID!
CAN YOU BE AT THE MILL TODAY, VIDIA?
FORGET IT, SWEET-TALKER!
SWEET-TALKER? I THOUGHT SHE LIKED HELPING...
I GUESS MY KINDNESS-PRACTICING PLAN FAILED!
WHAT'S WRONG WITH HER? SHE WAS ACTUALLY A BIG HELP...
HEE! HEE! NEVER MIND HER! I'LL FILL YOU IN ON EVERYTHING.
WELCOME BACK, VIDIA!
TODAY I WANT TO FLY FASTER THAN THE WIND!
ZOOM
THE END

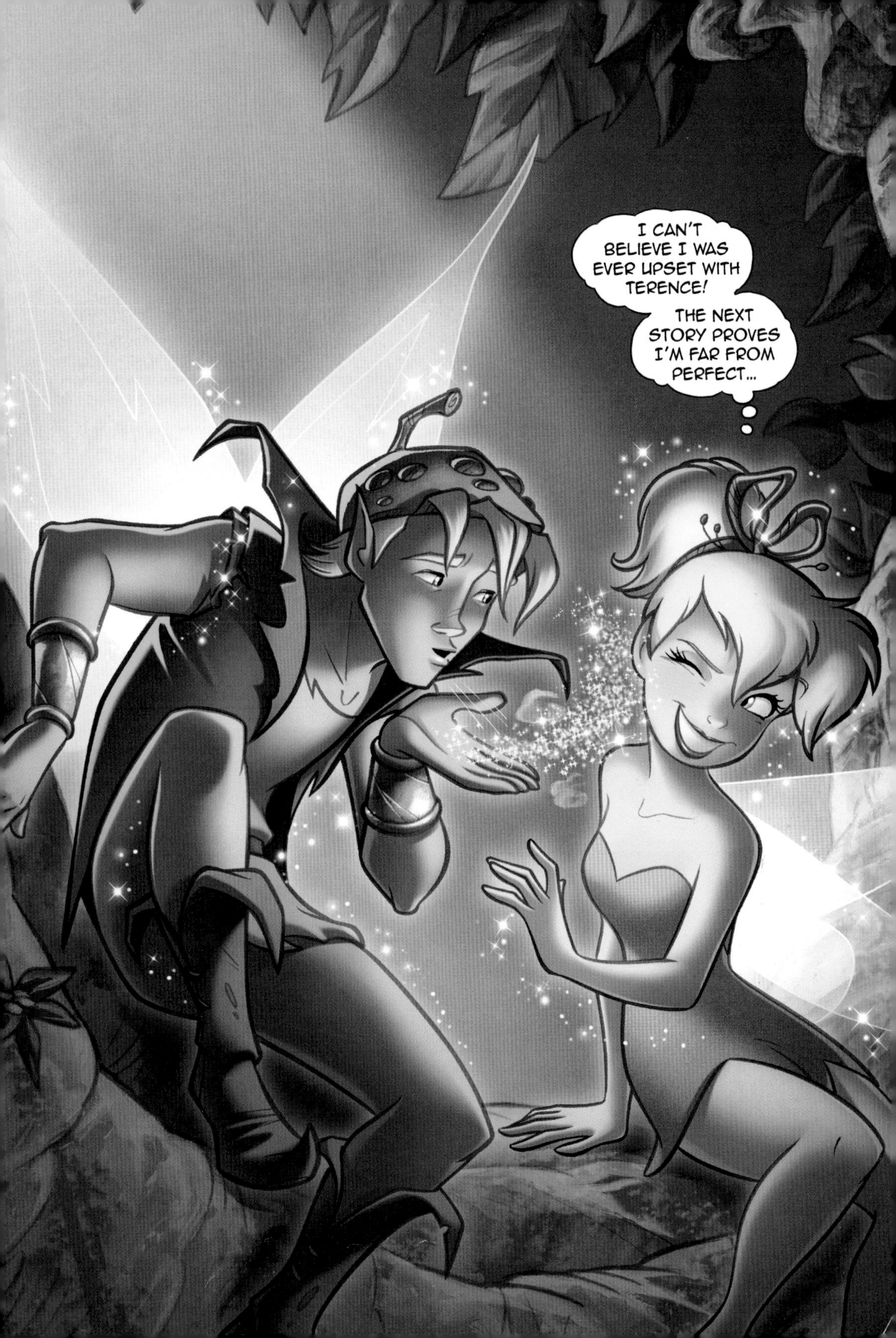
I CAN'T BELIEVE I WAS EVER UPSET WITH TERENCE!
THE NEXT STORY PROVES I'M FAR FROM PERFECT...

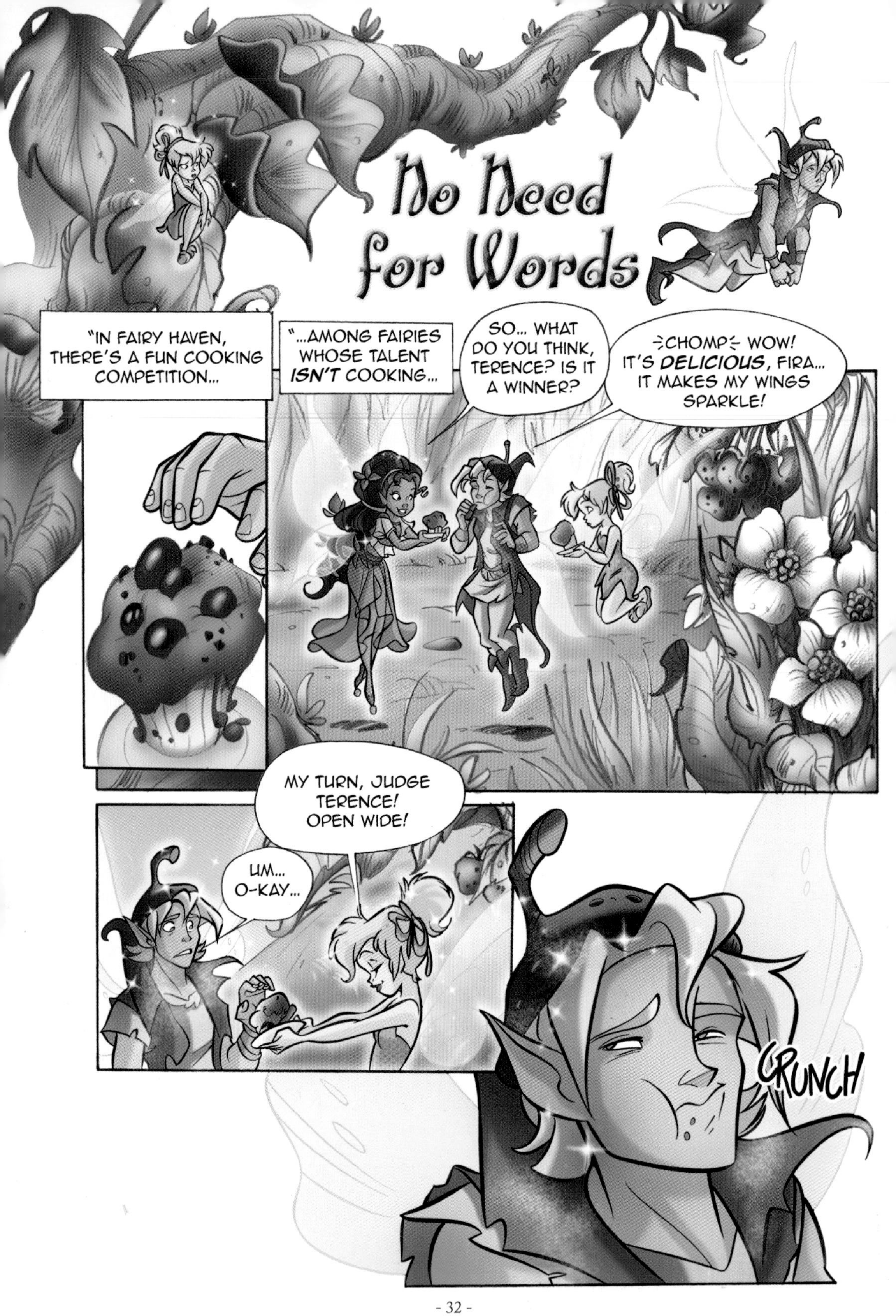
No Need for Words
"IN FAIRY HAVEN, THERE'S A FUN COOKING COMPETITION...
"...AMONG FAIRIES WHOSE TALENT ISN'T COOKING...
SO... WHAT DO YOU THINK, TERENCE? IS IT A WINNER?
CHOMP WOW! IT'S DELICIOUS, FIRA... IT MAKES MY WINGS SPARKLE!
MY TURN, JUDGE TERENCE! OPEN WIDE!
UM... O-KAY...
CRUNCH

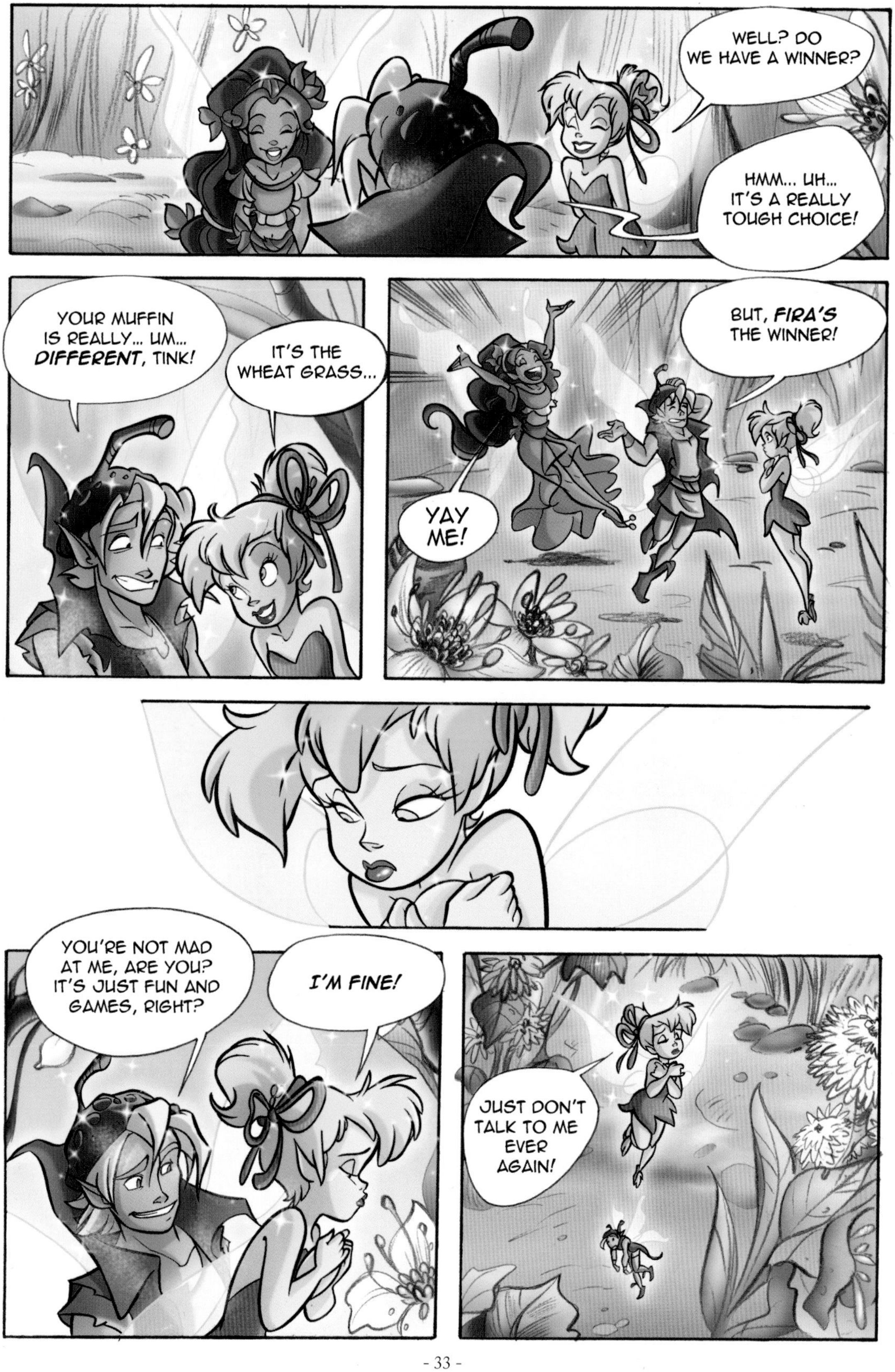
WELL? DO WE HAVE A WINNER?
HMM... UH... IT'S A REALLY TOUGH CHOICE!
YOUR MUFFIN IS REALLY... UM... **DIFFERENT**, TINK!
IT'S THE WHEAT GRASS...
BUT, ***FIRA'S*** THE WINNER!
YAY ME!
YOU'RE NOT MAD AT ME, ARE YOU? IT'S JUST FUN AND GAMES, RIGHT?
I'M FINE!
JUST DON'T TALK TO ME EVER AGAIN!

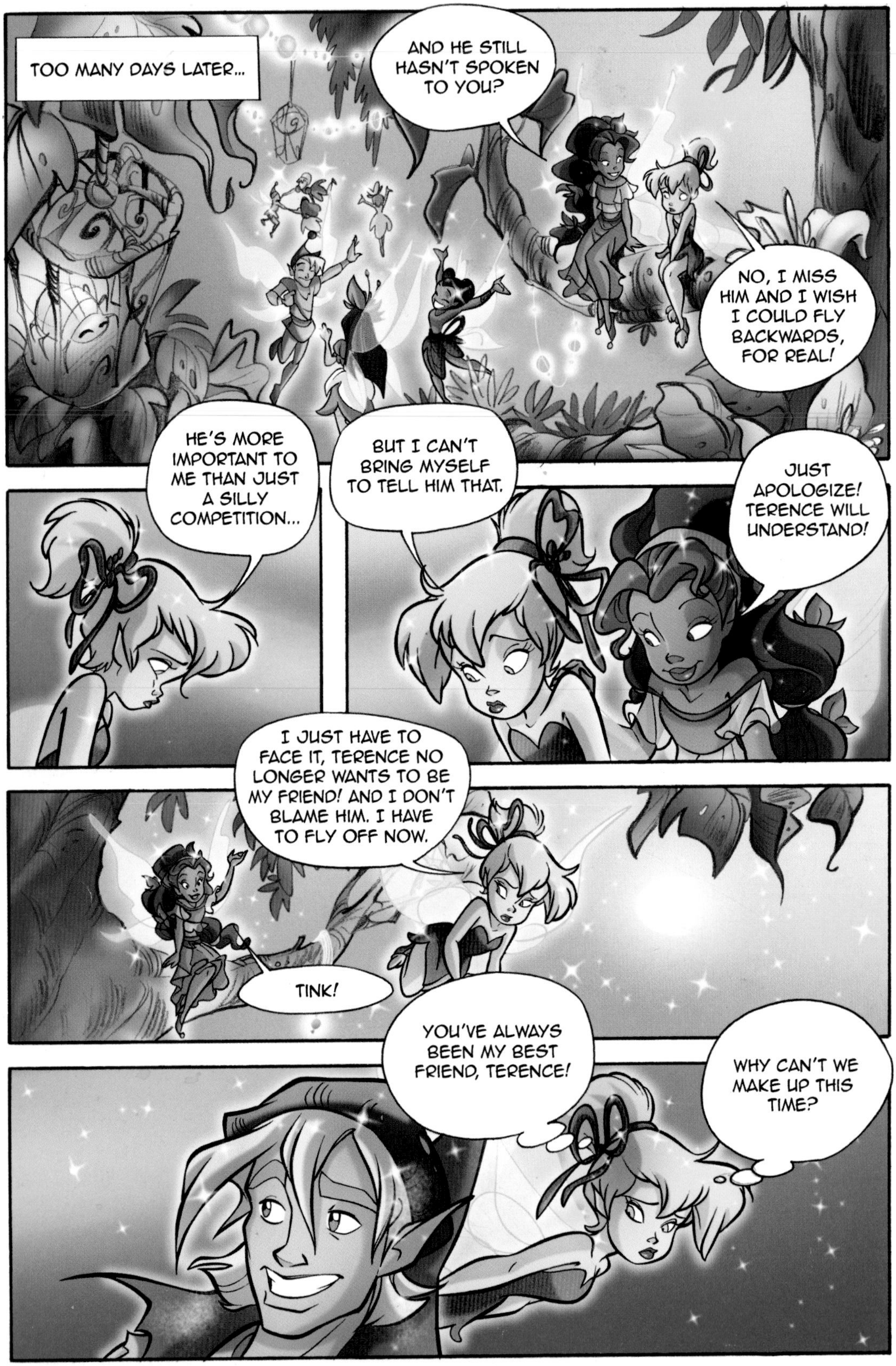
TOO MANY DAYS LATER...
AND HE STILL HASN'T SPOKEN TO YOU?
NO, I MISS HIM AND I WISH I COULD FLY BACKWARDS, FOR REAL!
HE'S MORE IMPORTANT TO ME THAN JUST A SILLY COMPETITION...
BUT I CAN'T BRING MYSELF TO TELL HIM THAT.
JUST APOLOGIZE! TERENCE WILL UNDERSTAND!
I JUST HAVE TO FACE IT, TERENCE NO LONGER WANTS TO BE MY FRIEND! AND I DON'T BLAME HIM. I HAVE TO FLY OFF NOW.
TINK!
YOU'VE ALWAYS BEEN MY BEST FRIEND, TERENCE!
WHY CAN'T WE MAKE UP THIS TIME?

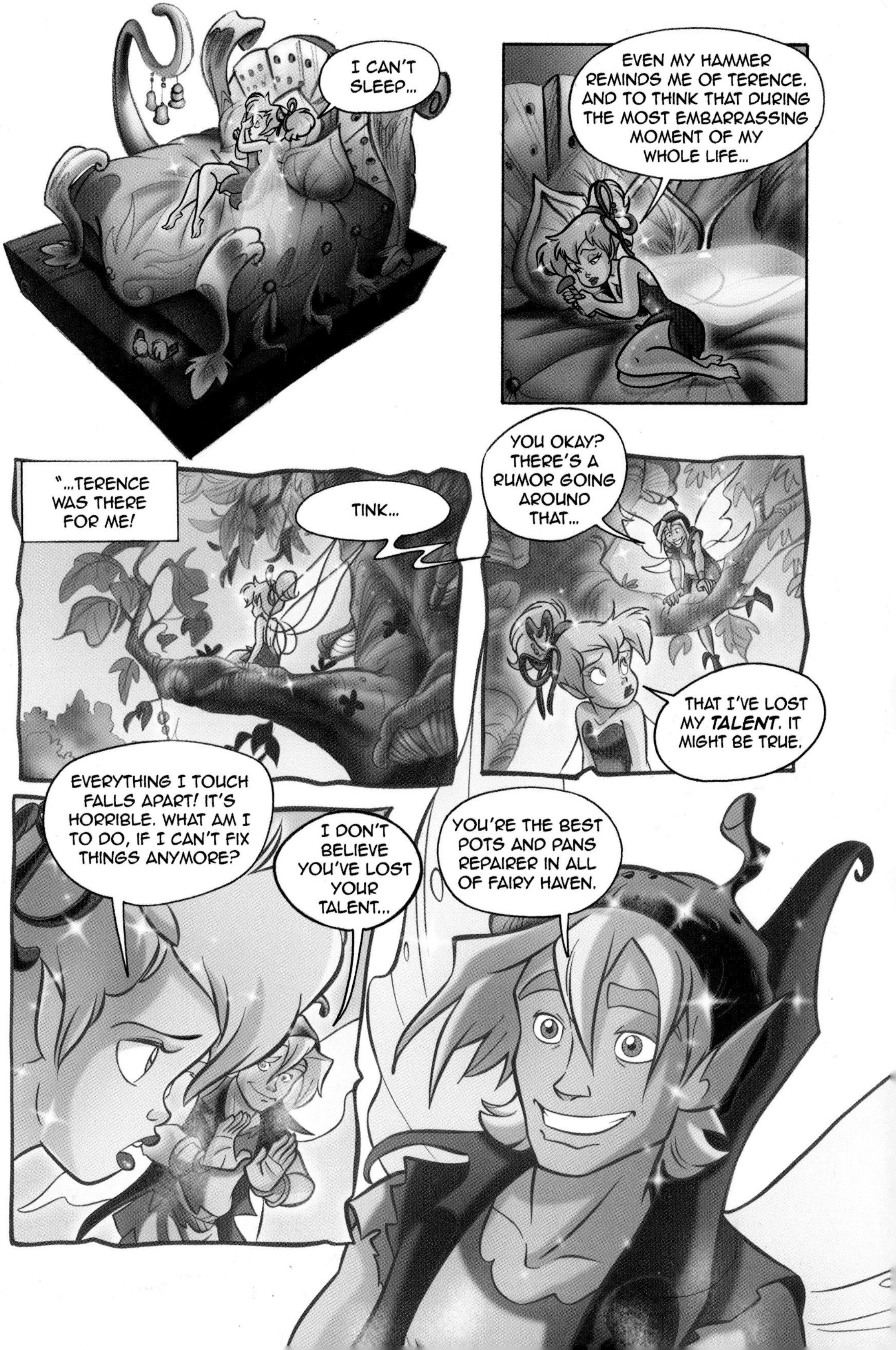

I CAN'T SLEEP...
EVEN MY HAMMER REMINDS ME OF TERENCE. AND TO THINK THAT DURING THE MOST EMBARRASSING MOMENT OF MY WHOLE LIFE...
"...TERENCE WAS THERE FOR ME!
TINK...
YOU OKAY? THERE'S A RUMOR GOING AROUND THAT...
THAT I'VE LOST MY *TALENT*. IT MIGHT BE TRUE.
EVERYTHING I TOUCH FALLS APART! IT'S HORRIBLE. WHAT AM I TO DO, IF I CAN'T FIX THINGS ANYMORE?
I DON'T BELIEVE YOU'VE LOST YOUR TALENT...
YOU'RE THE BEST POTS AND PANS REPAIRER IN ALL OF FAIRY HAVEN.

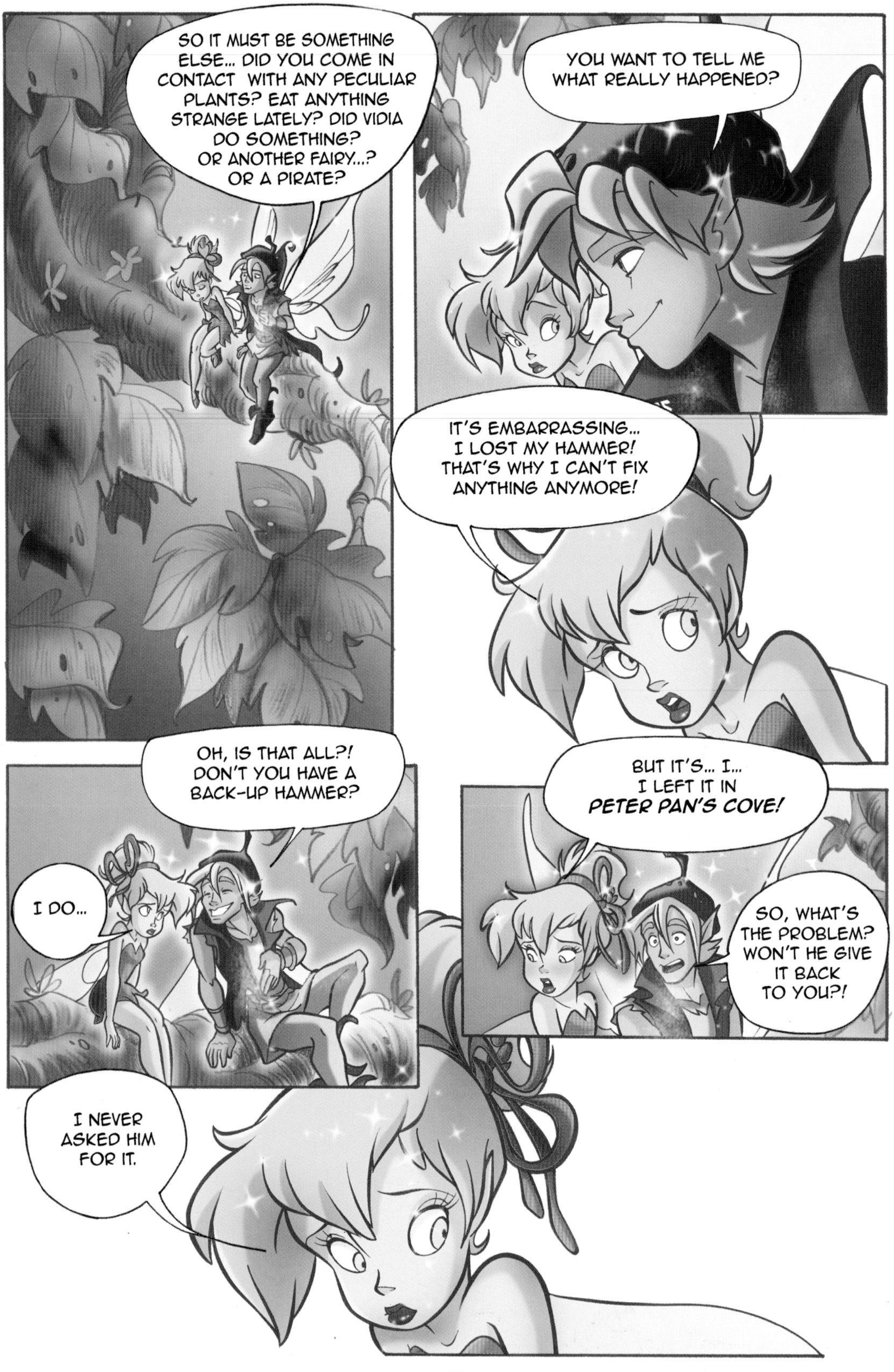
SO IT MUST BE SOMETHING ELSE... DID YOU COME IN CONTACT WITH ANY PECULIAR PLANTS? EAT ANYTHING STRANGE LATELY? DID VIDIA DO SOMETHING? OR ANOTHER FAIRY...? OR A PIRATE?
YOU WANT TO TELL ME WHAT REALLY HAPPENED?
IT'S EMBARRASSING... I LOST MY HAMMER! THAT'S WHY I CAN'T FIX ANYTHING ANYMORE!
OH, IS THAT ALL?! DON'T YOU HAVE A BACK-UP HAMMER?
I DO...
BUT IT'S... I... I LEFT IT IN *PETER PAN'S COVE!*
SO, WHAT'S THE PROBLEM? WON'T HE GIVE IT BACK TO YOU?!
I NEVER ASKED HIM FOR IT.

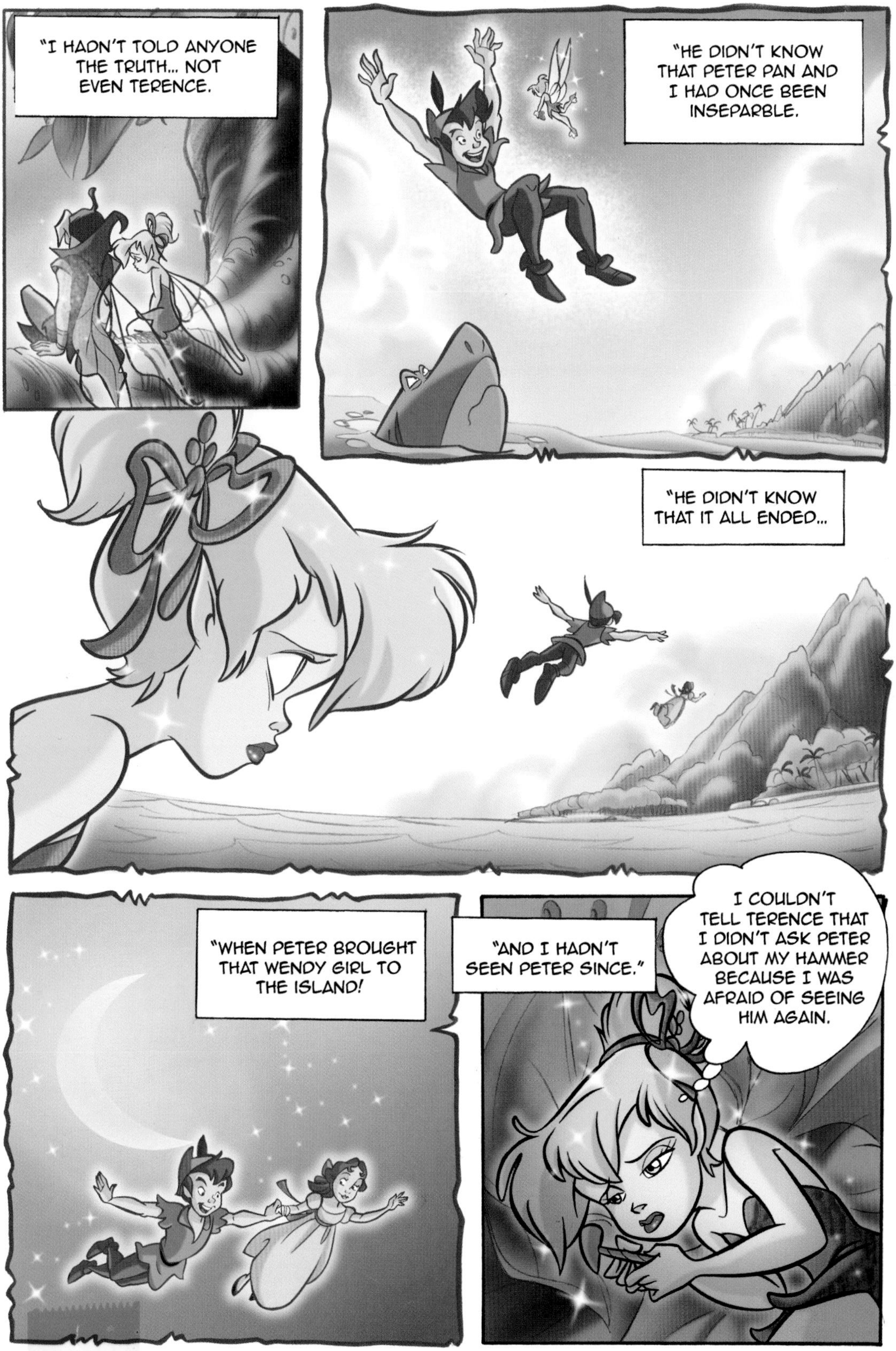
"I HADN'T TOLD ANYONE THE TRUTH... NOT EVEN TERENCE.
"HE DIDN'T KNOW THAT PETER PAN AND I HAD ONCE BEEN INSEPARBLE.
"HE DIDN'T KNOW THAT IT ALL ENDED...
"WHEN PETER BROUGHT THAT WENDY GIRL TO THE ISLAND!
"AND I HADN'T SEEN PETER SINCE."
I COULDN'T TELL TERENCE THAT I DIDN'T ASK PETER ABOUT MY HAMMER BECAUSE I WAS AFRAID OF SEEING HIM AGAIN.

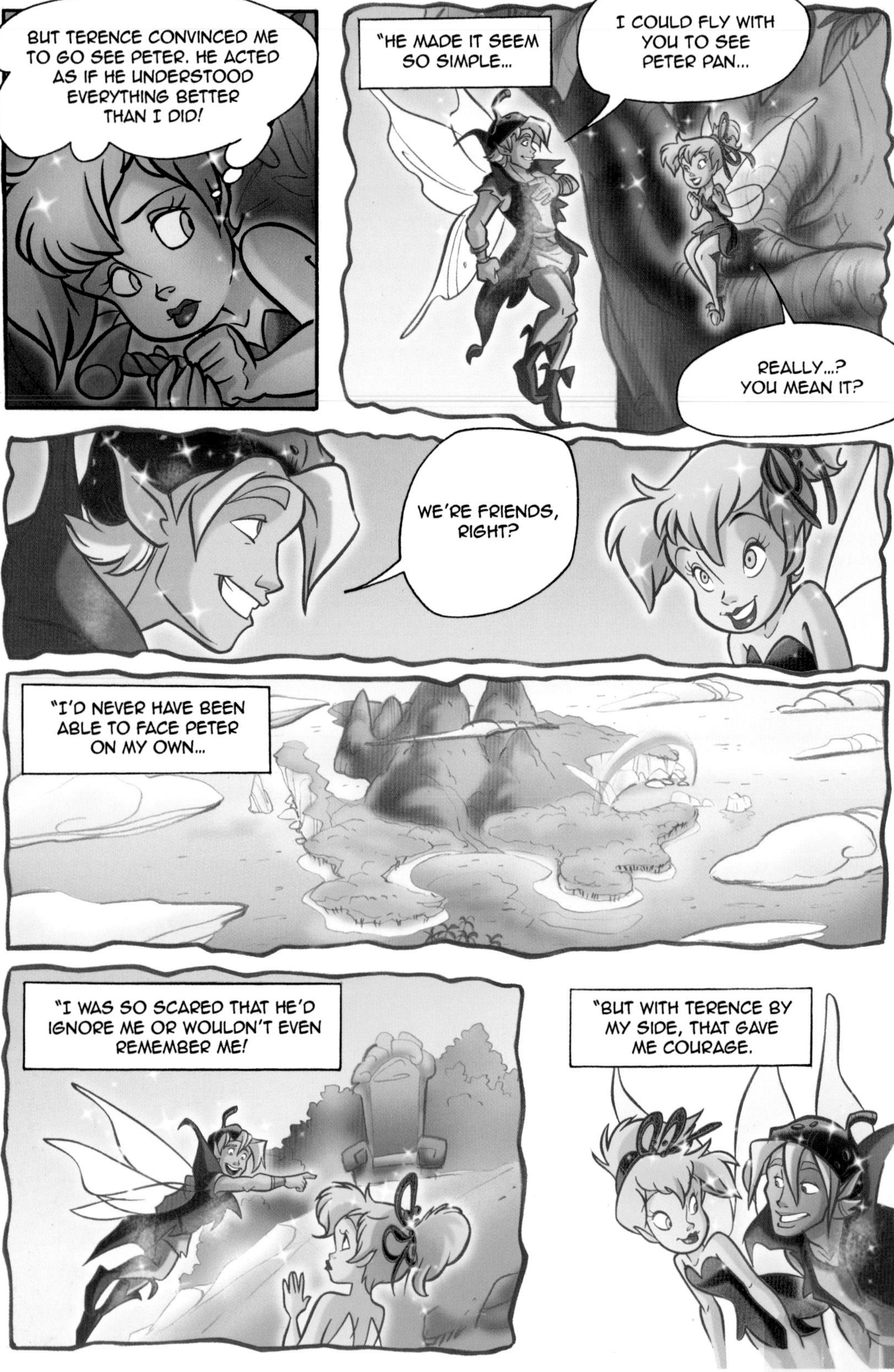
BUT TERENCE CONVINCED ME TO GO SEE PETER. HE ACTED AS IF HE UNDERSTOOD EVERYTHING BETTER THAN I DID!
"HE MADE IT SEEM SO SIMPLE...
I COULD FLY WITH YOU TO SEE PETER PAN...
REALLY...? YOU MEAN IT?
WE'RE FRIENDS, RIGHT?
"I'D NEVER HAVE BEEN ABLE TO FACE PETER ON MY OWN...
"I WAS SO SCARED THAT HE'D IGNORE ME OR WOULDN'T EVEN REMEMBER ME!
"BUT WITH TERENCE BY MY SIDE, THAT GAVE ME COURAGE.

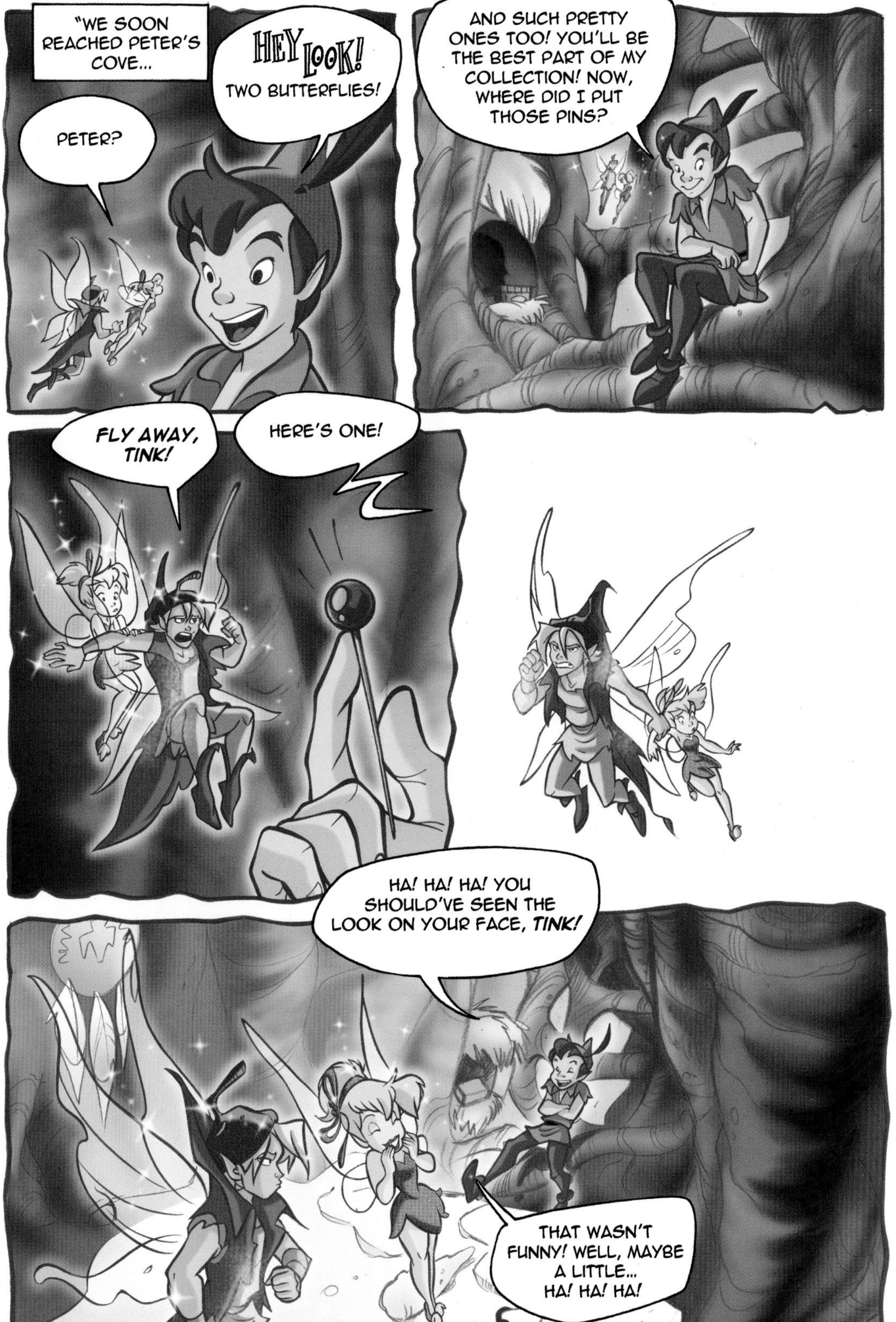
"WE SOON REACHED PETER'S COVE...
HEY LOOK! TWO BUTTERFLIES!
PETER?
AND SUCH PRETTY ONES TOO! YOU'LL BE THE BEST PART OF MY COLLECTION! NOW, WHERE DID I PUT THOSE PINS?
FLY AWAY, TINK!
HERE'S ONE!
HA! HA! HA! YOU SHOULD'VE SEEN THE LOOK ON YOUR FACE, TINK!
THAT WASN'T FUNNY! WELL, MAYBE A LITTLE... HA! HA! HA!

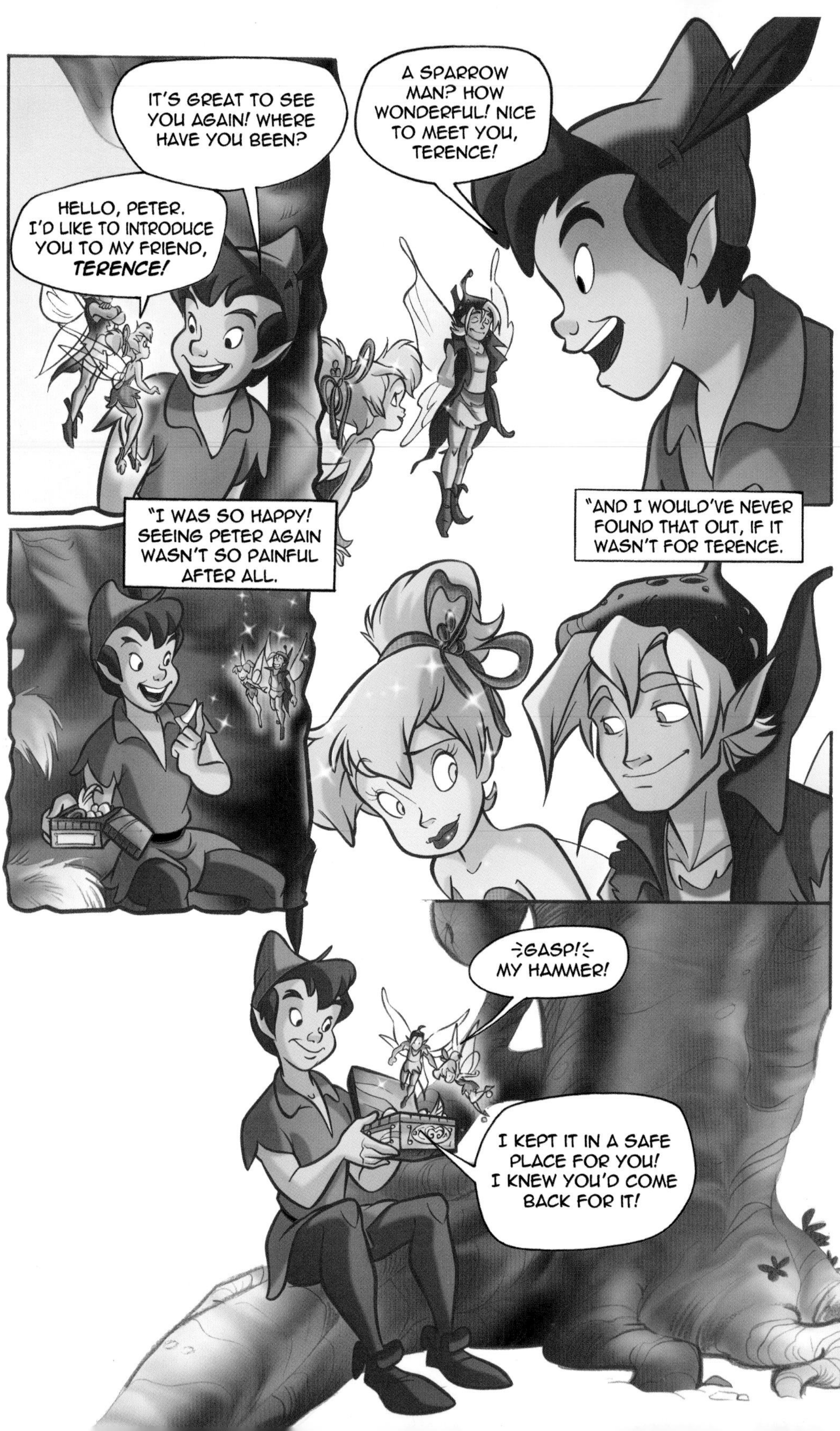
HELLO, PETER. I'D LIKE TO INTRODUCE YOU TO MY FRIEND, *TERENCE!*
IT'S GREAT TO SEE YOU AGAIN! WHERE HAVE YOU BEEN?
A SPARROW MAN? HOW WONDERFUL! NICE TO MEET YOU, TERENCE!
"I WAS SO HAPPY! SEEING PETER AGAIN WASN'T SO PAINFUL AFTER ALL.
"AND I WOULD'VE NEVER FOUND THAT OUT, IF IT WASN'T FOR TERENCE.
GASP! MY HAMMER!
I KEPT IT IN A SAFE PLACE FOR YOU! I KNEW YOU'D COME BACK FOR IT!

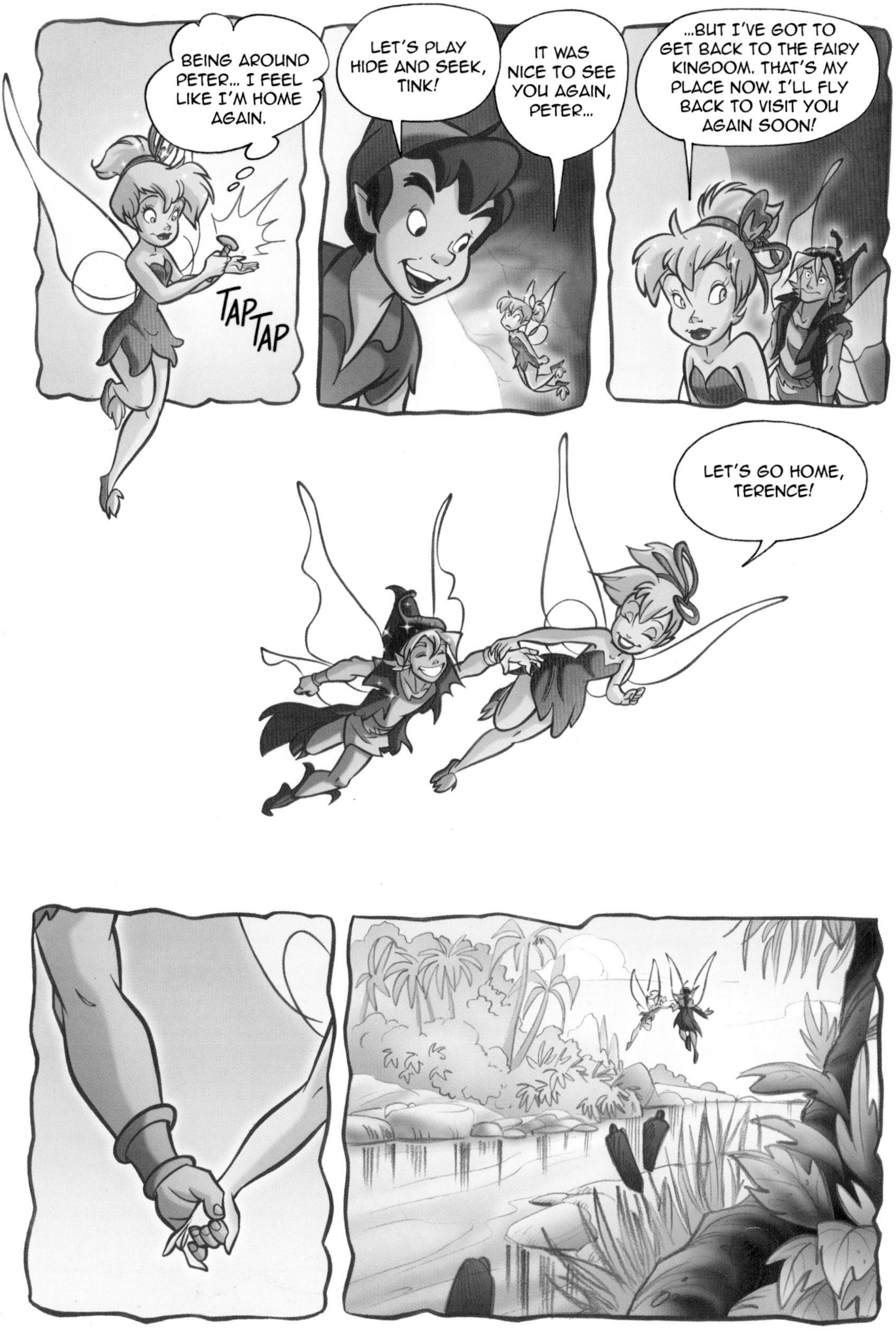
BEING AROUND PETER... I FEEL LIKE I'M HOME AGAIN.
TAP TAP
LET'S PLAY HIDE AND SEEK, TINK!
IT WAS NICE TO SEE YOU AGAIN, PETER...
...BUT I'VE GOT TO GET BACK TO THE FAIRY KINGDOM. THAT'S MY PLACE NOW. I'LL FLY BACK TO VISIT YOU AGAIN SOON!
LET'S GO HOME, TERENCE!

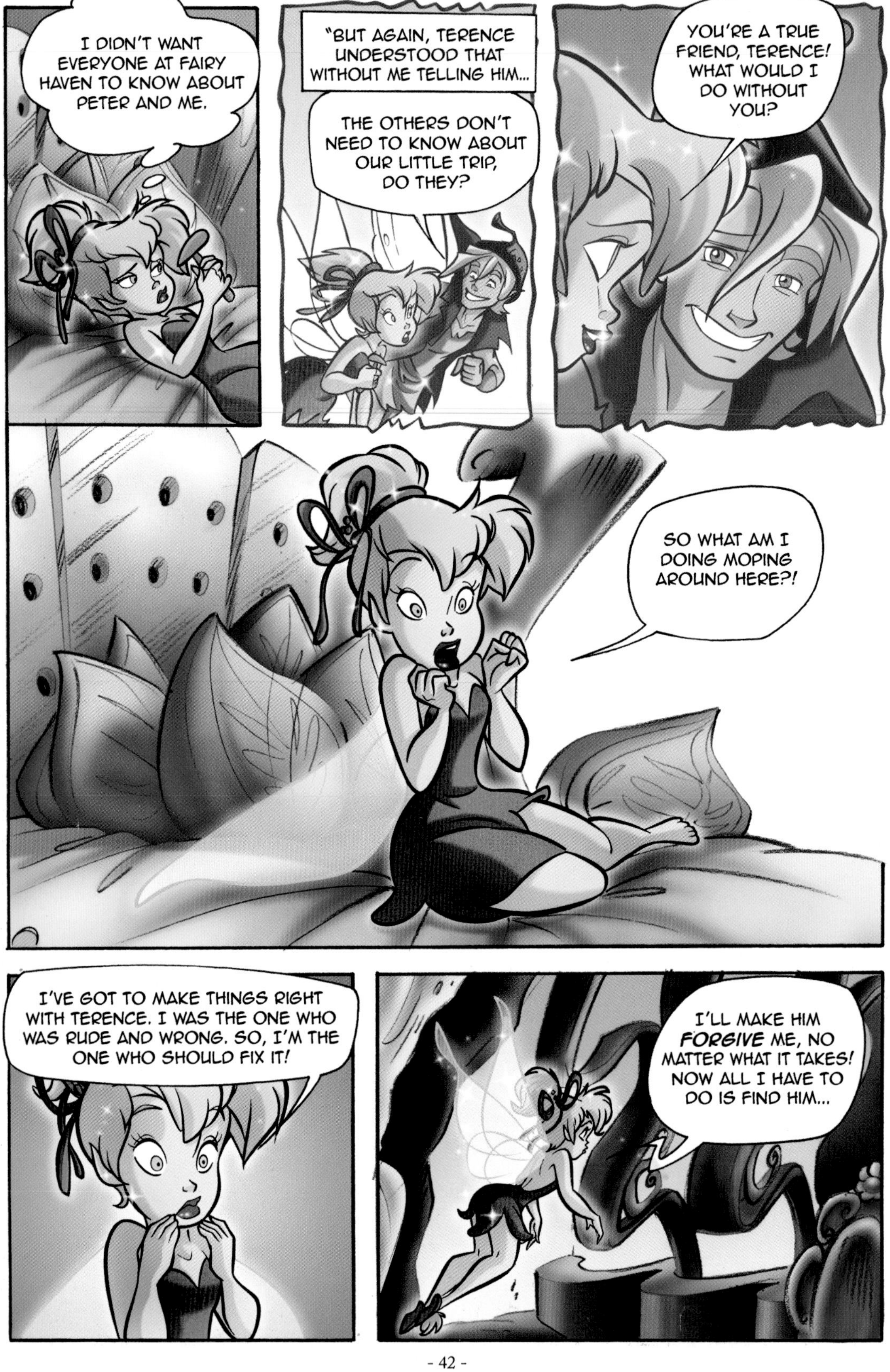
I DIDN'T WANT EVERYONE AT FAIRY HAVEN TO KNOW ABOUT PETER AND ME.
"BUT AGAIN, TERENCE UNDERSTOOD THAT WITHOUT ME TELLING HIM...
THE OTHERS DON'T NEED TO KNOW ABOUT OUR LITTLE TRIP, DO THEY?
YOU'RE A TRUE FRIEND, TERENCE! WHAT WOULD I DO WITHOUT YOU?
SO WHAT AM I DOING MOPING AROUND HERE?!
I'VE GOT TO MAKE THINGS RIGHT WITH TERENCE. I WAS THE ONE WHO WAS RUDE AND WRONG. SO, I'M THE ONE WHO SHOULD FIX IT!
I'LL MAKE HIM *FORGIVE* ME, NO MATTER WHAT IT TAKES! NOW ALL I HAVE TO DO IS FIND HIM...

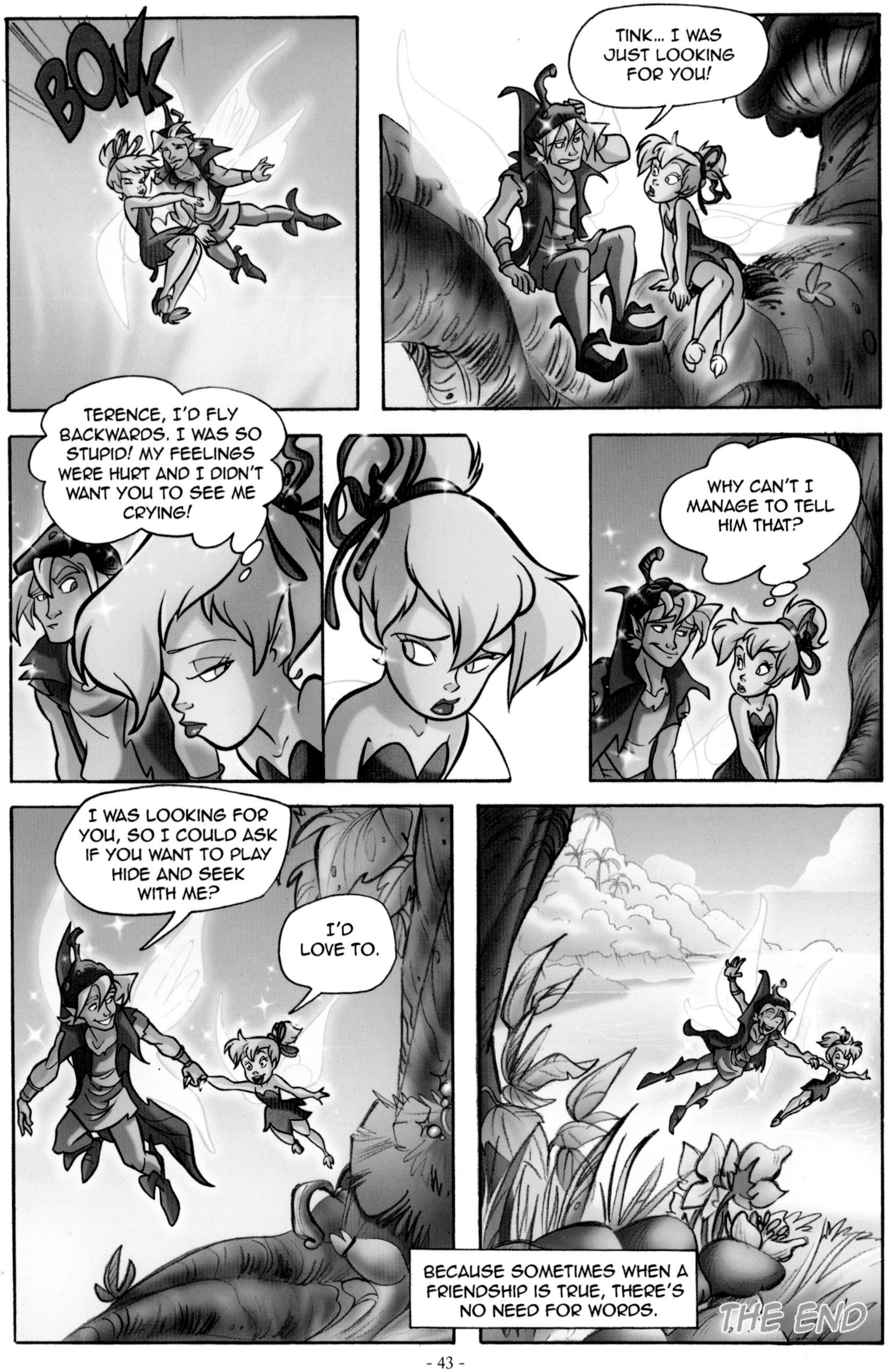

BONK
TINK... I WAS JUST LOOKING FOR YOU!
TERENCE, I'D FLY BACKWARDS. I WAS SO STUPID! MY FEELINGS WERE HURT AND I DIDN'T WANT YOU TO SEE ME CRYING!
WHY CAN'T I MANAGE TO TELL HIM THAT?
I WAS LOOKING FOR YOU, SO I COULD ASK IF YOU WANT TO PLAY HIDE AND SEEK WITH ME?
I'D LOVE TO.
BECAUSE SOMETIMES WHEN A FRIENDSHIP IS TRUE, THERE'S NO NEED FOR WORDS.
THE END

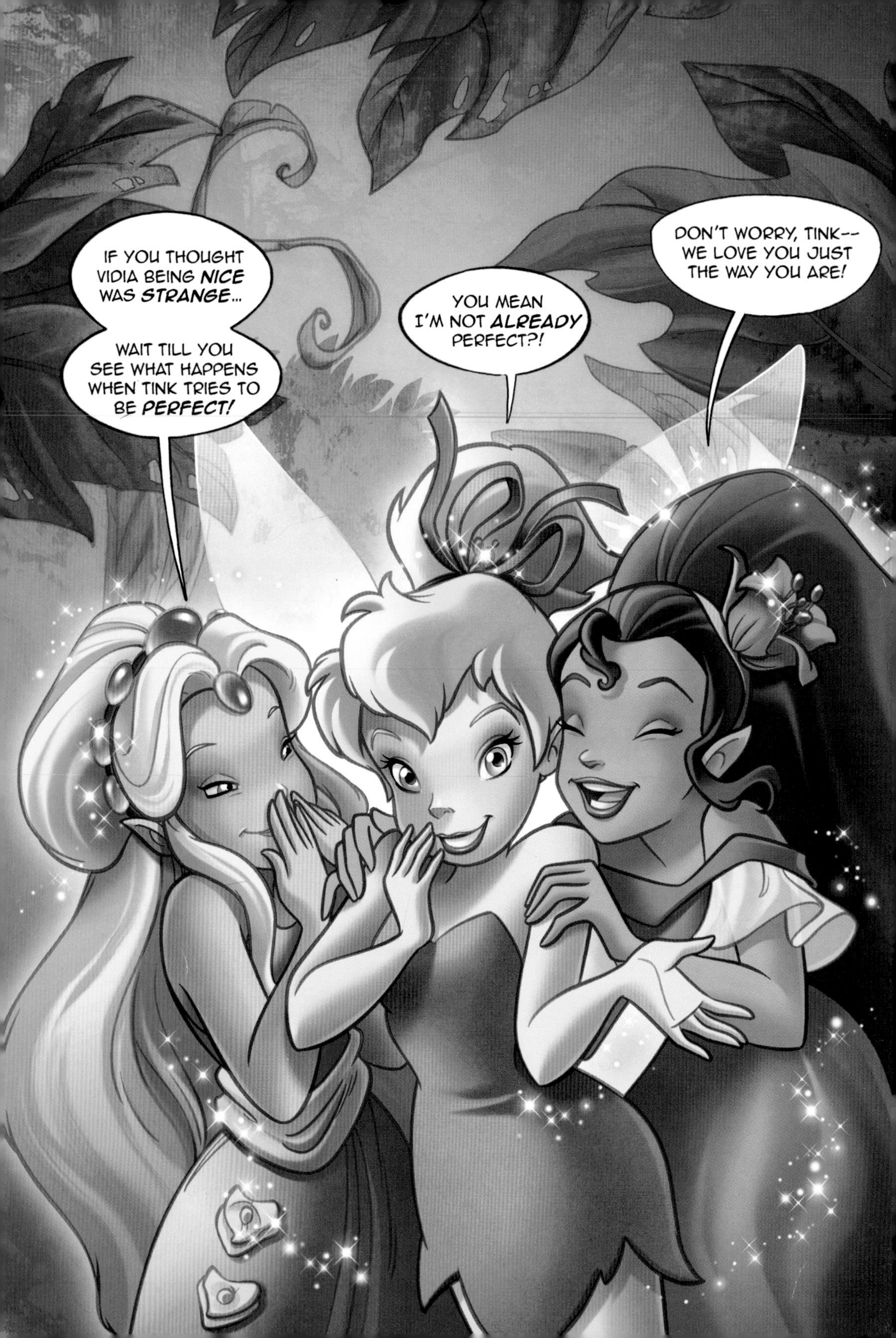
IF YOU THOUGHT VIDIA BEING NICE WAS STRANGE...
WAIT TILL YOU SEE WHAT HAPPENS WHEN TINK TRIES TO BE PERFECT!
YOU MEAN I'M NOT ALREADY PERFECT?!
DON'T WORRY, TINK-- WE LOVE YOU JUST THE WAY YOU ARE!

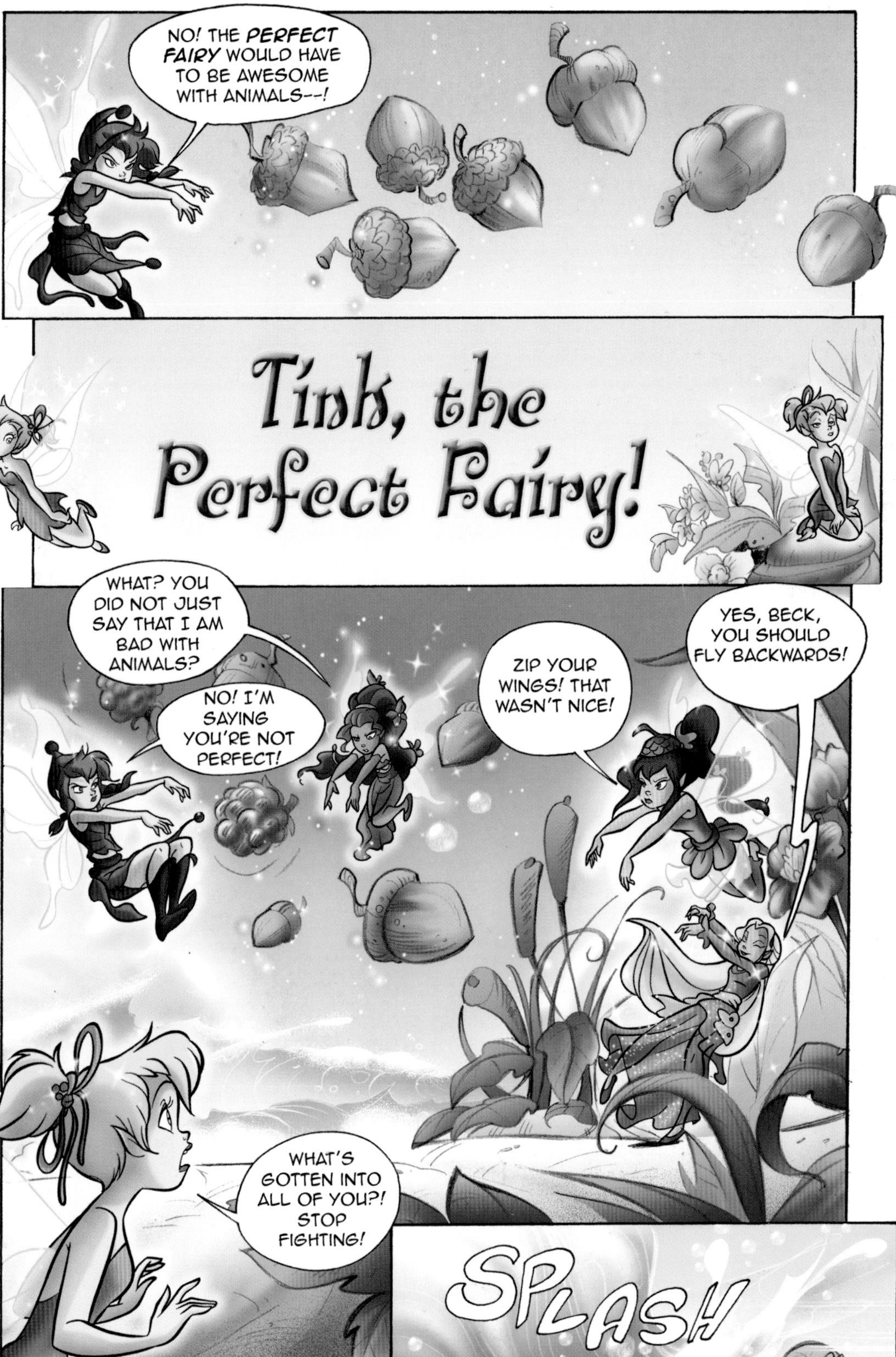
NO! THE PERFECT FAIRY WOULD HAVE TO BE AWESOME WITH ANIMALS--!
Tink, the Perfect Fairy!
WHAT? YOU DID NOT JUST SAY THAT I AM BAD WITH ANIMALS?
NO! I'M SAYING YOU'RE NOT PERFECT!
ZIP YOUR WINGS! THAT WASN'T NICE!
YES, BECK, YOU SHOULD FLY BACKWARDS!
WHAT'S GOTTEN INTO ALL OF YOU?! STOP FIGHTING!
SPLASH

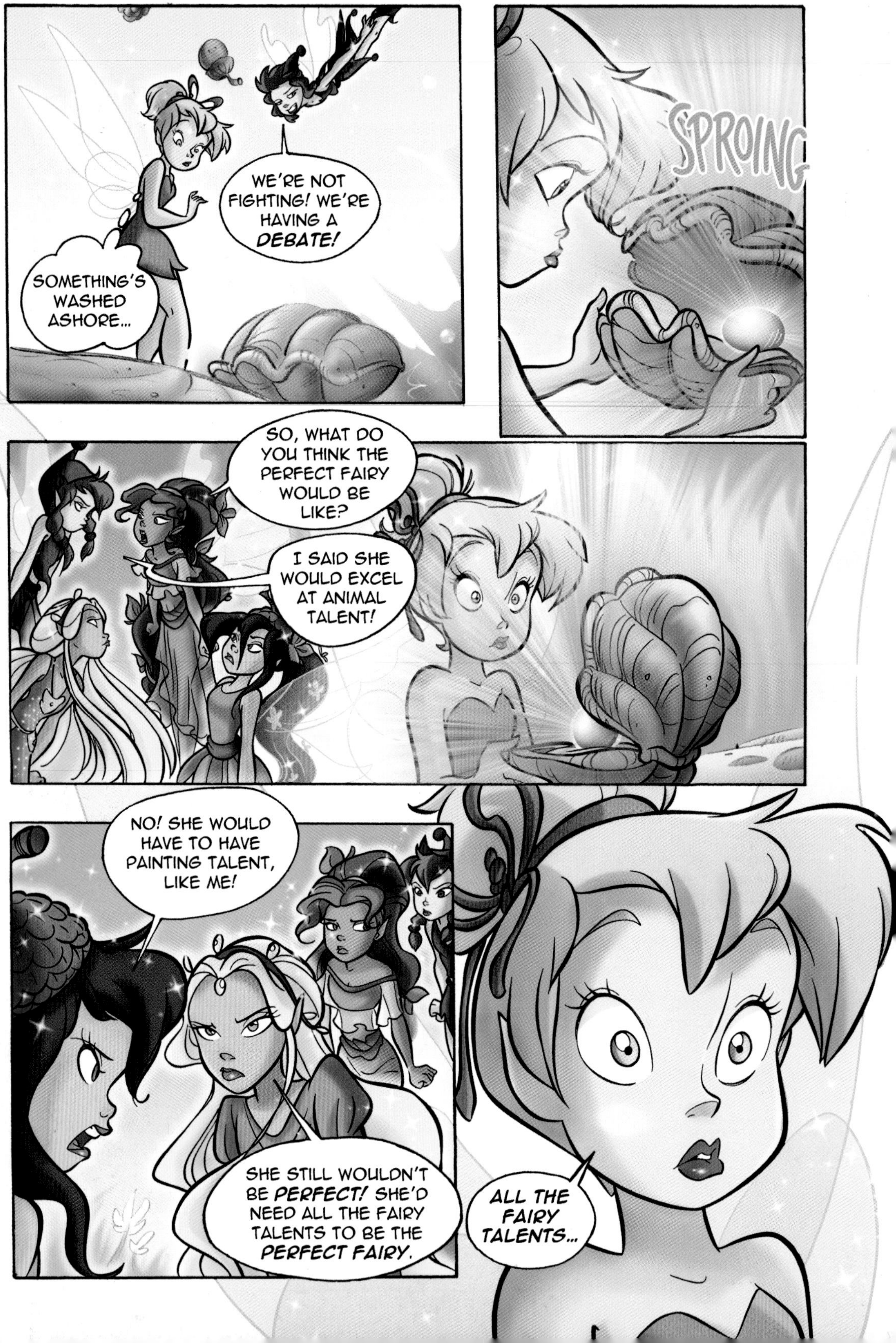
SOMETHING'S WASHED ASHORE...
WE'RE NOT FIGHTING! WE'RE HAVING A *DEBATE!*
SPROING
SO, WHAT DO YOU THINK THE PERFECT FAIRY WOULD BE LIKE?
I SAID SHE WOULD EXCEL AT ANIMAL TALENT!
NO! SHE WOULD HAVE TO HAVE PAINTING TALENT, LIKE ME!
SHE STILL WOULDN'T BE *PERFECT!* SHE'D NEED ALL THE FAIRY TALENTS TO BE THE *PERFECT FAIRY*.
ALL THE FAIRY TALENTS...

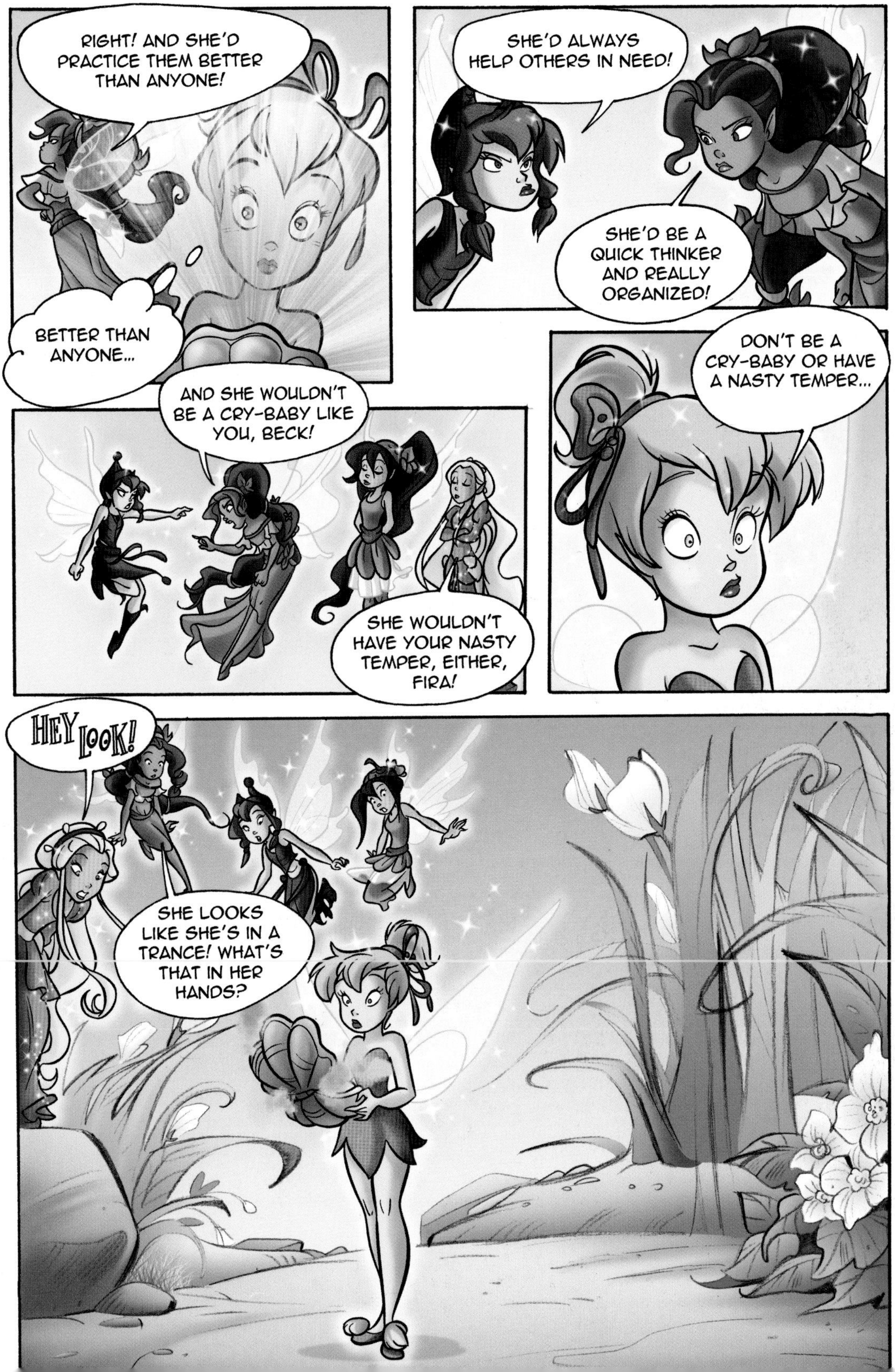
RIGHT! AND SHE'D PRACTICE THEM BETTER THAN ANYONE!
BETTER THAN ANYONE...
SHE'D ALWAYS HELP OTHERS IN NEED!
SHE'D BE A QUICK THINKER AND REALLY ORGANIZED!
AND SHE WOULDN'T BE A CRY-BABY LIKE YOU, BECK!
SHE WOULDN'T HAVE YOUR NASTY TEMPER, EITHER, FIRA!
DON'T BE A CRY-BABY OR HAVE A NASTY TEMPER...
HEY LOOK!
SHE LOOKS LIKE SHE'S IN A TRANCE! WHAT'S THAT IN HER HANDS?

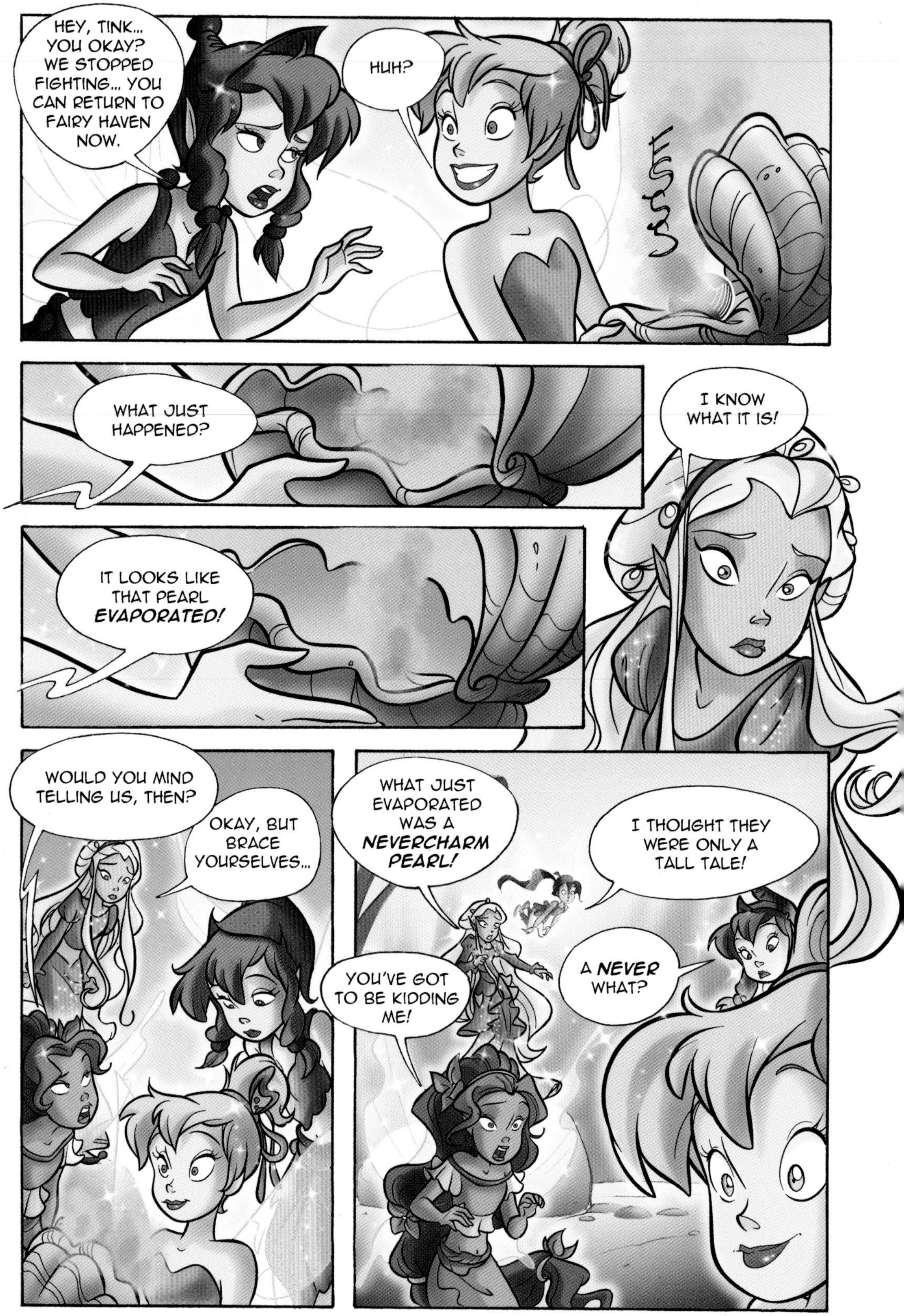
HEY, TINK... YOU OKAY? WE STOPPED FIGHTING... YOU CAN RETURN TO FAIRY HAVEN NOW.
HUH?
WHAT JUST HAPPENED?
I KNOW WHAT IT IS!
IT LOOKS LIKE THAT PEARL *EVAPORATED!*
WOULD YOU MIND TELLING US, THEN?
OKAY, BUT BRACE YOURSELVES...
WHAT JUST EVAPORATED WAS A *NEVERCHARM PEARL!*
I THOUGHT THEY WERE ONLY A TALL TALE!
YOU'VE GOT TO BE KIDDING ME!
A *NEVER* WHAT?

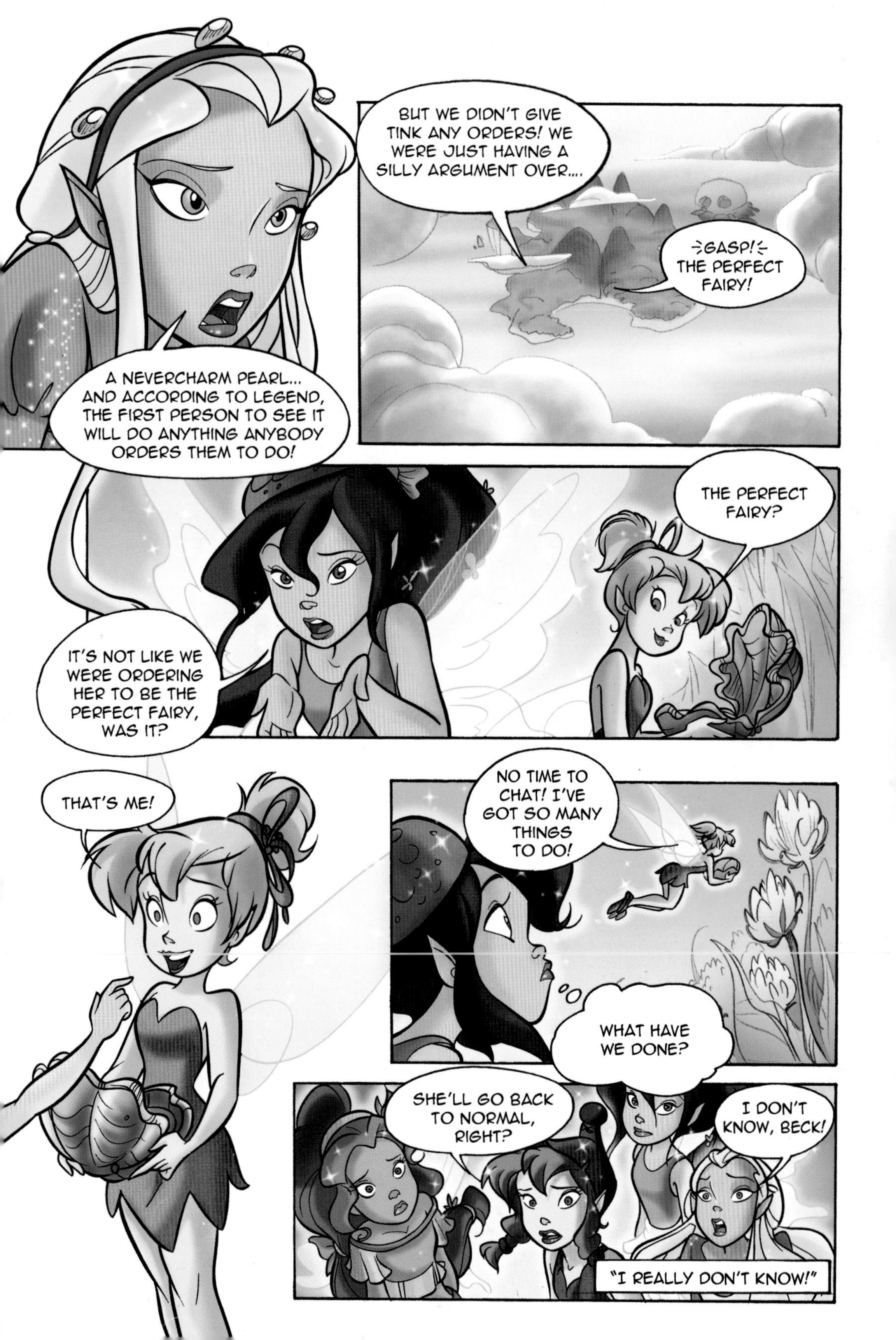
A NEVERCHARM PEARL... AND ACCORDING TO LEGEND, THE FIRST PERSON TO SEE IT WILL DO ANYTHING ANYBODY ORDERS THEM TO DO!
BUT WE DIDN'T GIVE TINK ANY ORDERS! WE WERE JUST HAVING A SILLY ARGUMENT OVER....
GASP! THE PERFECT FAIRY!
IT'S NOT LIKE WE WERE ORDERING HER TO BE THE PERFECT FAIRY, WAS IT?
THE PERFECT FAIRY?
THAT'S ME!
NO TIME TO CHAT! I'VE GOT SO MANY THINGS TO DO!
WHAT HAVE WE DONE?
SHE'LL GO BACK TO NORMAL, RIGHT?
I DON'T KNOW, BECK!
"I REALLY DON'T KNOW!"

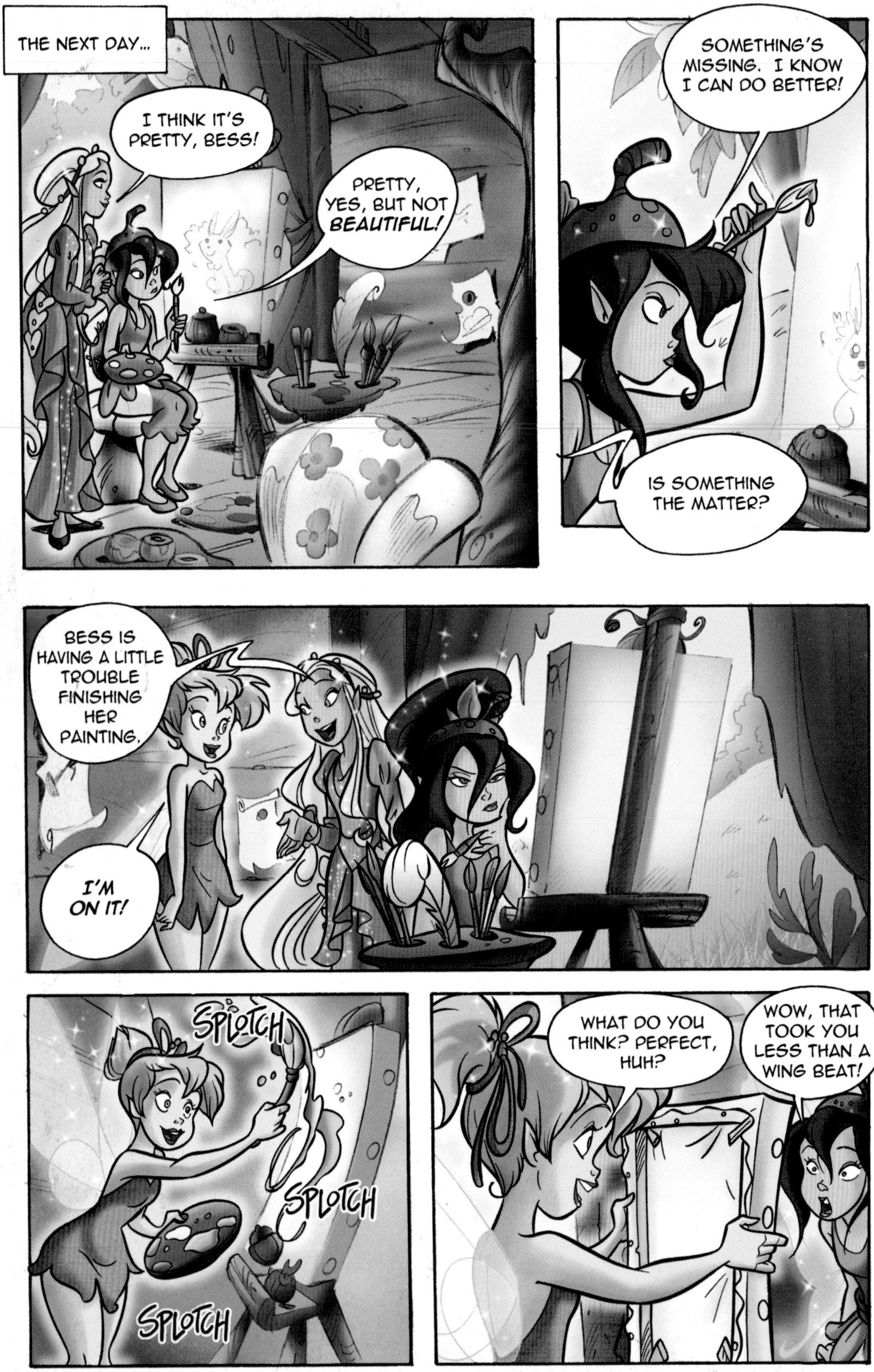
THE NEXT DAY...
I THINK IT'S PRETTY, BESS!
PRETTY, YES, BUT NOT BEAUTIFUL!
SOMETHING'S MISSING. I KNOW I CAN DO BETTER!
IS SOMETHING THE MATTER?
BESS IS HAVING A LITTLE TROUBLE FINISHING HER PAINTING.
I'M ON IT!
SPLOTCH
SPLOTCH
SPLOTCH
WHAT DO YOU THINK? PERFECT, HUH?
WOW, THAT TOOK YOU LESS THAN A WING BEAT!

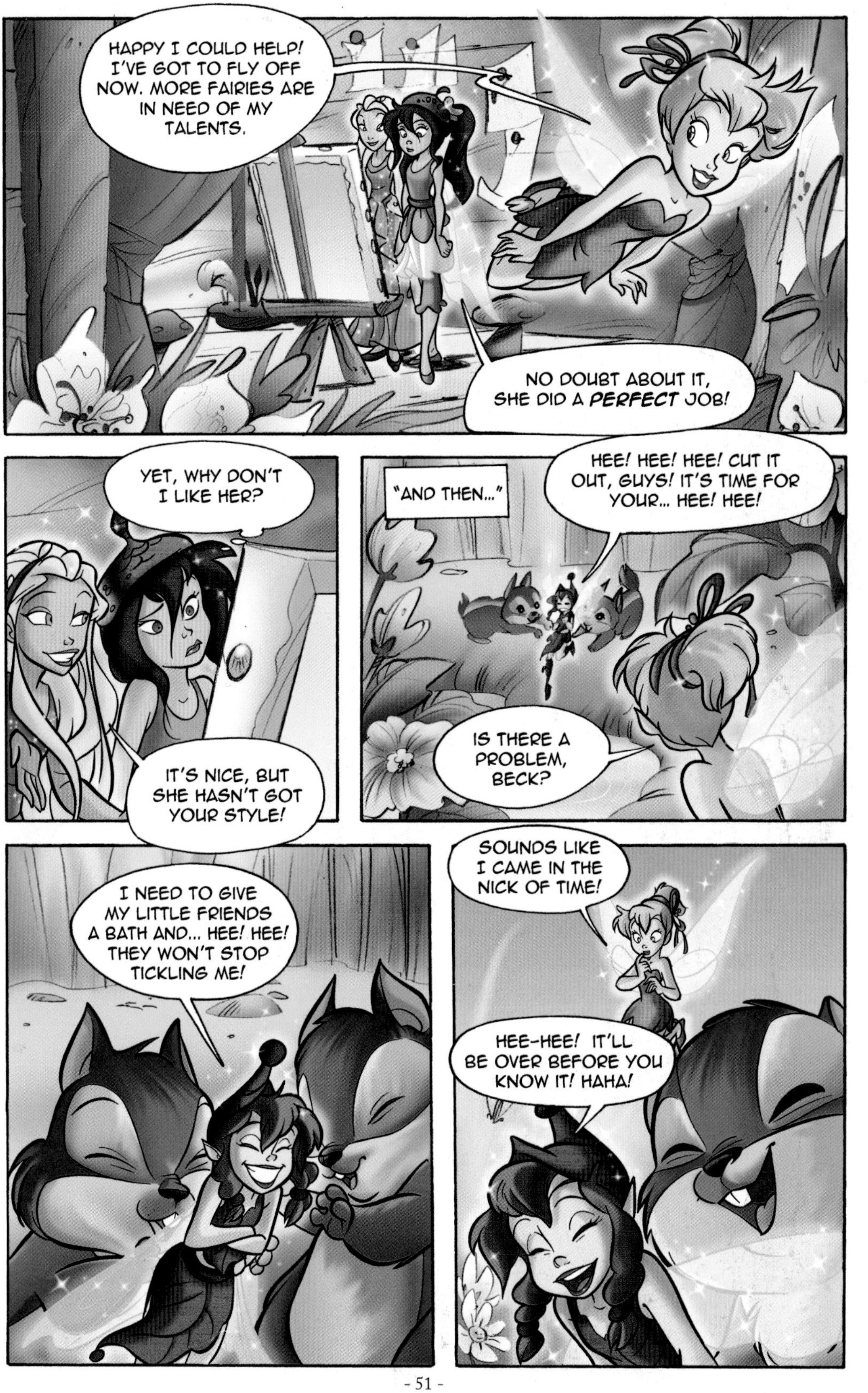
HAPPY I COULD HELP! I'VE GOT TO FLY OFF NOW. MORE FAIRIES ARE IN NEED OF MY TALENTS.
NO DOUBT ABOUT IT, SHE DID A *PERFECT* JOB!
YET, WHY DON'T I LIKE HER?
IT'S NICE, BUT SHE HASN'T GOT YOUR STYLE!
"AND THEN..."
HEE! HEE! HEE! CUT IT OUT, GUYS! IT'S TIME FOR YOUR... HEE! HEE!
IS THERE A PROBLEM, BECK?
I NEED TO GIVE MY LITTLE FRIENDS A BATH AND... HEE! HEE! THEY WON'T STOP TICKLING ME!
SOUNDS LIKE I CAME IN THE NICK OF TIME!
HEE-HEE! IT'LL BE OVER BEFORE YOU KNOW IT! HAHA!

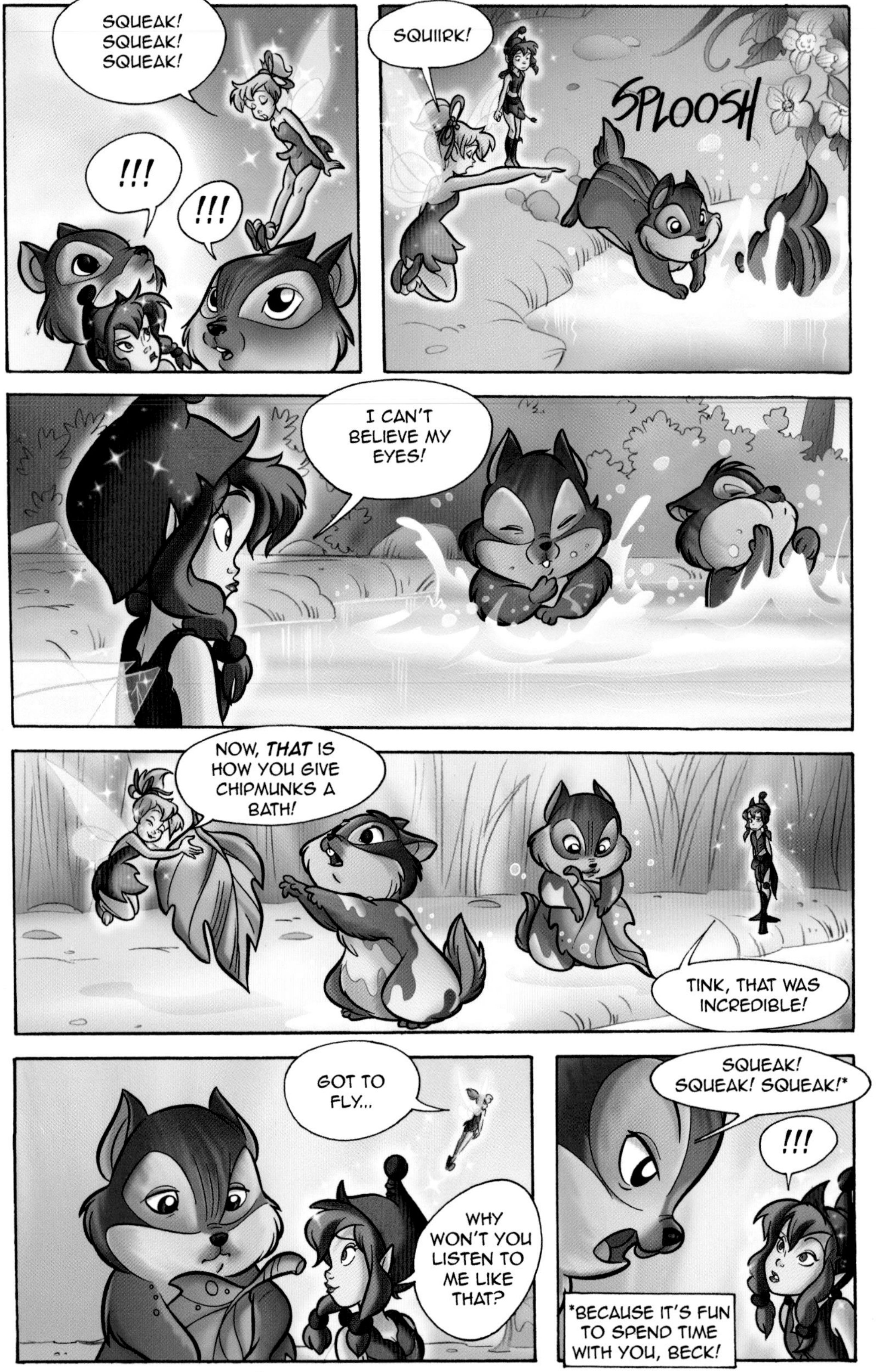
SQUEAK!
SQUEAK!
SQUEAK!
!!!
!!!
SQUIIRK!
SPLOOSH
I CAN'T BELIEVE MY EYES!
NOW, *THAT* IS HOW YOU GIVE CHIPMUNKS A BATH!
TINK, THAT WAS INCREDIBLE!
GOT TO FLY...
WHY WON'T YOU LISTEN TO ME LIKE THAT?
SQUEAK! SQUEAK! SQUEAK!*
!!!
*BECAUSE IT'S FUN TO SPEND TIME WITH YOU, BECK!

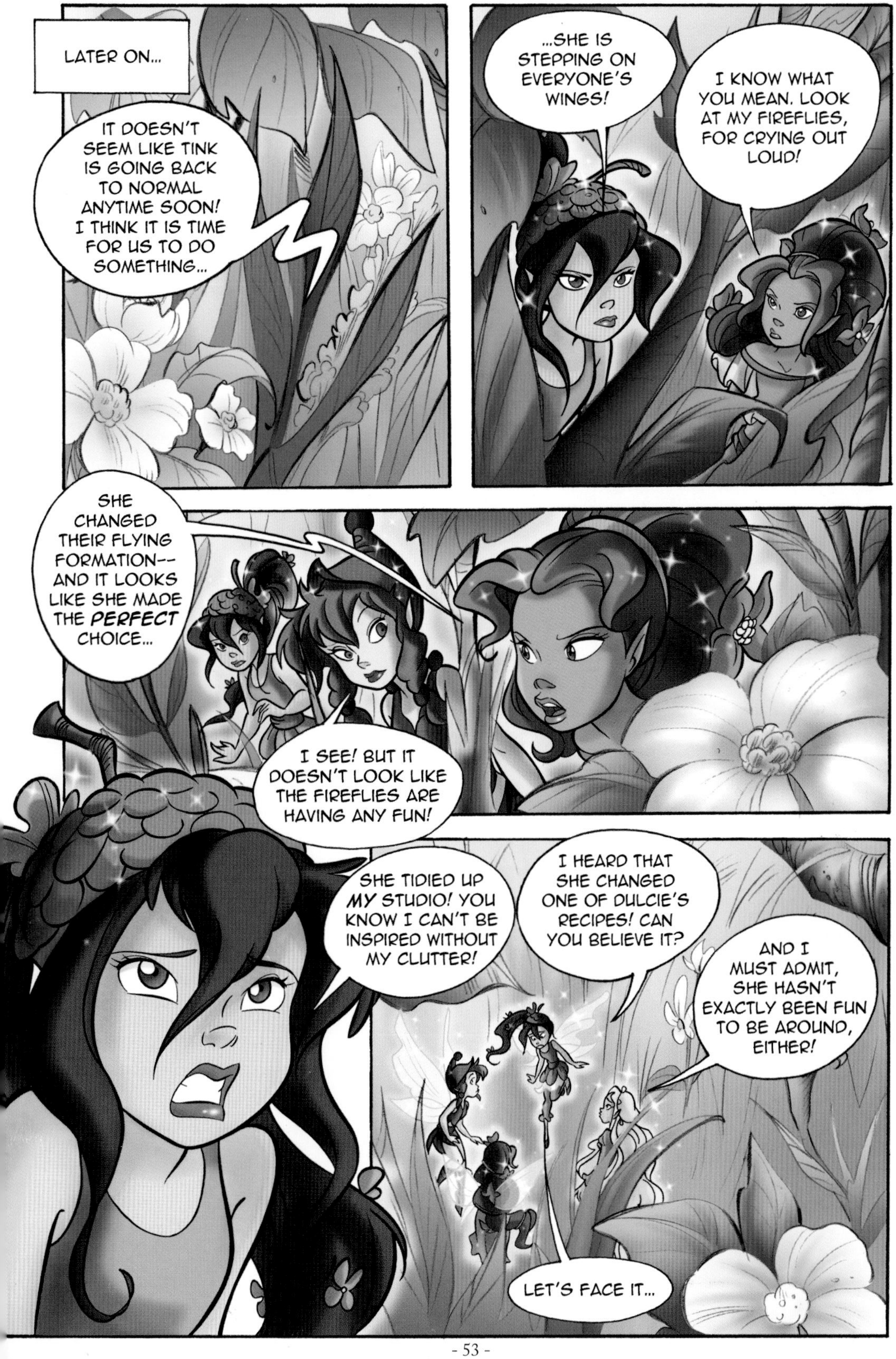
LATER ON...
IT DOESN'T SEEM LIKE TINK IS GOING BACK TO NORMAL ANYTIME SOON! I THINK IT IS TIME FOR US TO DO SOMETHING...
...SHE IS STEPPING ON EVERYONE'S WINGS!
I KNOW WHAT YOU MEAN. LOOK AT MY FIREFLIES, FOR CRYING OUT LOUD!
SHE CHANGED THEIR FLYING FORMATION-- AND IT LOOKS LIKE SHE MADE THE *PERFECT* CHOICE...
I SEE! BUT IT DOESN'T LOOK LIKE THE FIREFLIES ARE HAVING ANY FUN!
SHE TIDIED UP *MY* STUDIO! YOU KNOW I CAN'T BE INSPIRED WITHOUT MY CLUTTER!
I HEARD THAT SHE CHANGED ONE OF DULCIE'S RECIPES! CAN YOU BELIEVE IT?
AND I MUST ADMIT, SHE HASN'T EXACTLY BEEN FUN TO BE AROUND, EITHER!
LET'S FACE IT...

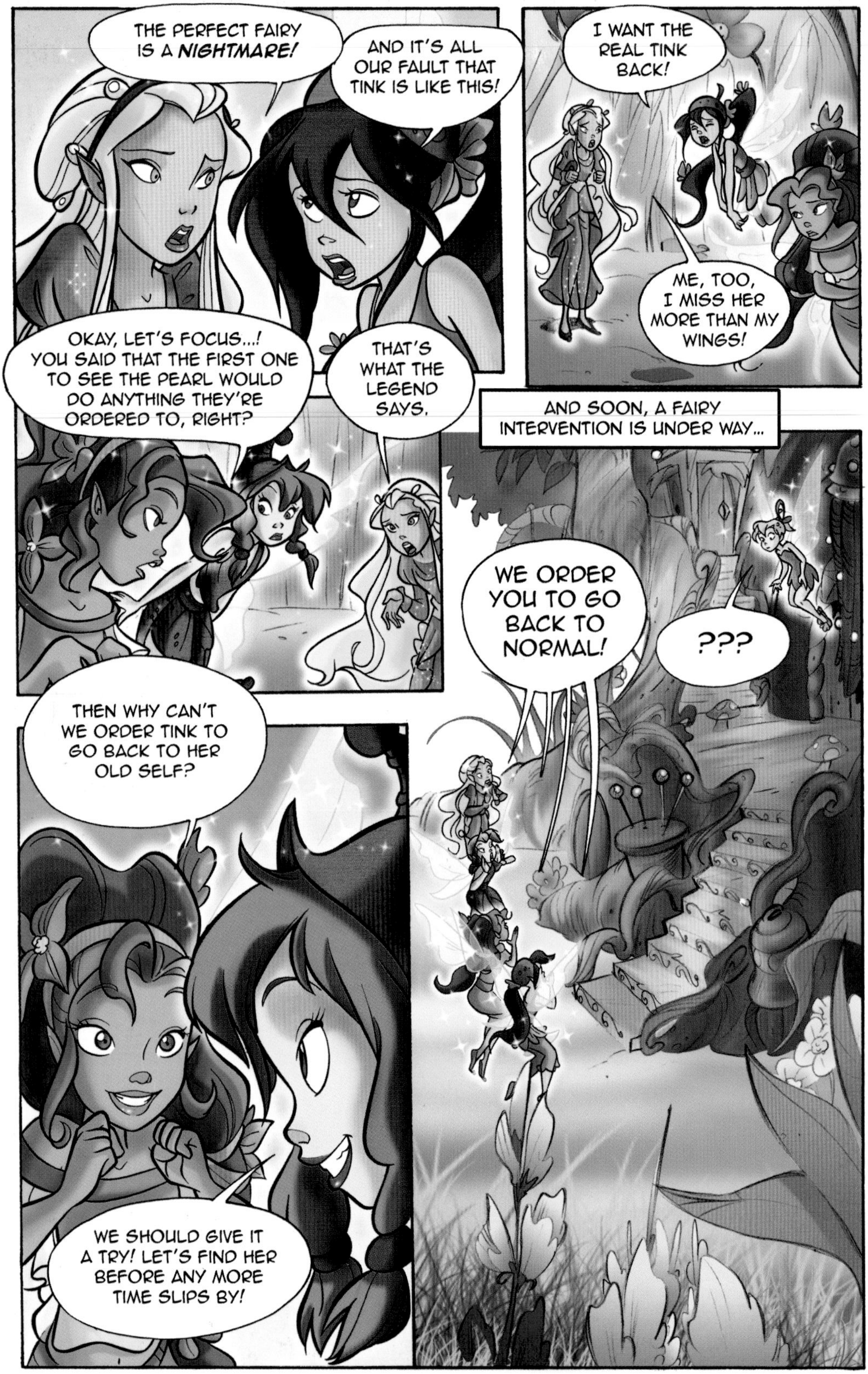

THE PERFECT FAIRY IS A *NIGHTMARE!*
AND IT'S ALL OUR FAULT THAT TINK IS LIKE THIS!
I WANT THE REAL TINK BACK!
ME, TOO, I MISS HER MORE THAN MY WINGS!
OKAY, LET'S FOCUS...! YOU SAID THAT THE FIRST ONE TO SEE THE PEARL WOULD DO ANYTHING THEY'RE ORDERED TO, RIGHT?
THAT'S WHAT THE LEGEND SAYS.
THEN WHY CAN'T WE ORDER TINK TO GO BACK TO HER OLD SELF?
WE SHOULD GIVE IT A TRY! LET'S FIND HER BEFORE ANY MORE TIME SLIPS BY!
AND SOON, A FAIRY INTERVENTION IS UNDER WAY...
WE ORDER YOU TO GO BACK TO NORMAL!
???

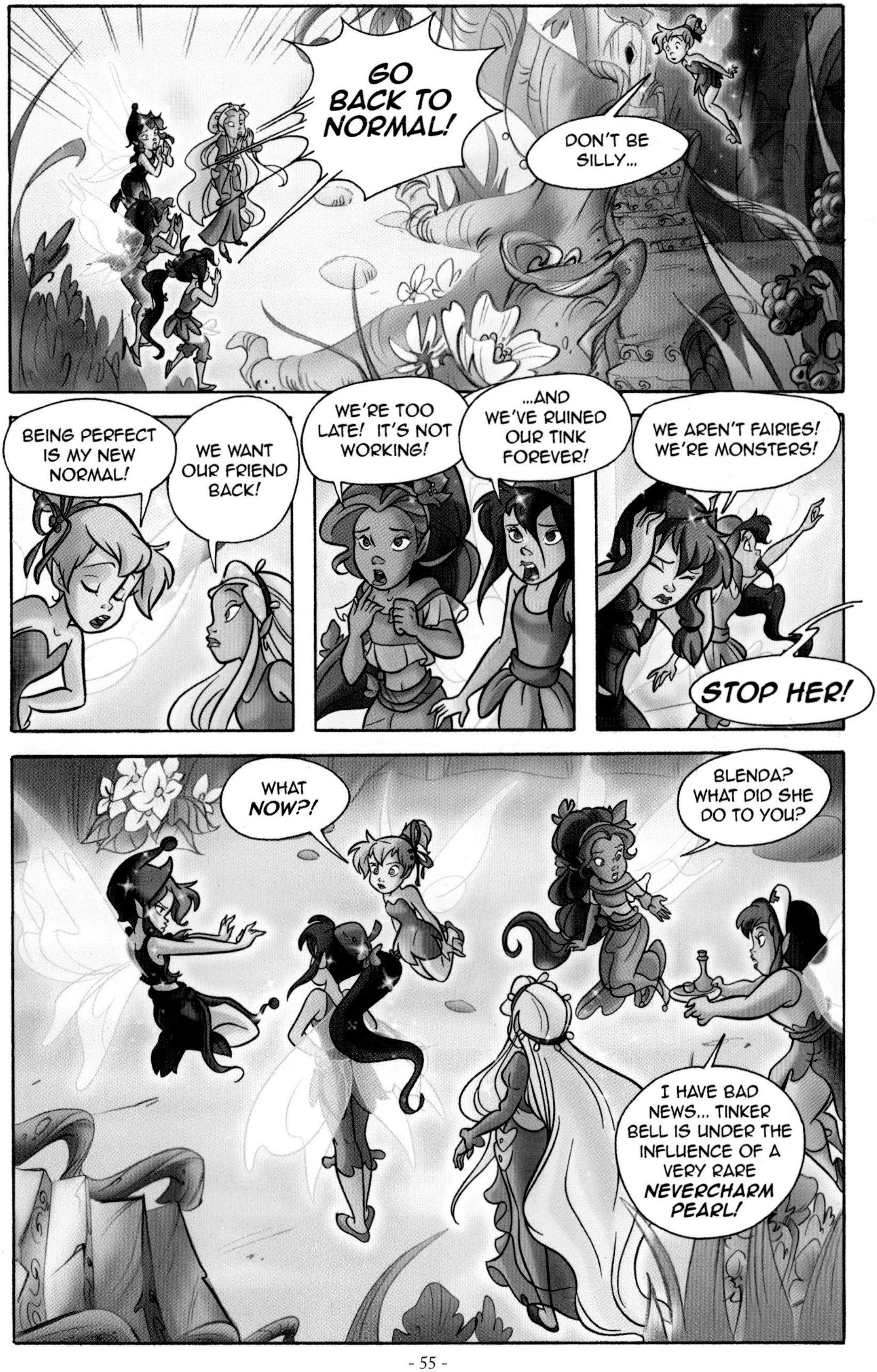
GO BACK TO NORMAL!
DON'T BE SILLY...
BEING PERFECT IS MY NEW NORMAL!
WE WANT OUR FRIEND BACK!
WE'RE TOO LATE! IT'S NOT WORKING!
...AND WE'VE RUINED OUR TINK FOREVER!
WE AREN'T FAIRIES! WE'RE MONSTERS!
STOP HER!
WHAT NOW?!
BLENDA? WHAT DID SHE DO TO YOU?
I HAVE BAD NEWS... TINKER BELL IS UNDER THE INFLUENCE OF A VERY RARE NEVERCHARM PEARL!

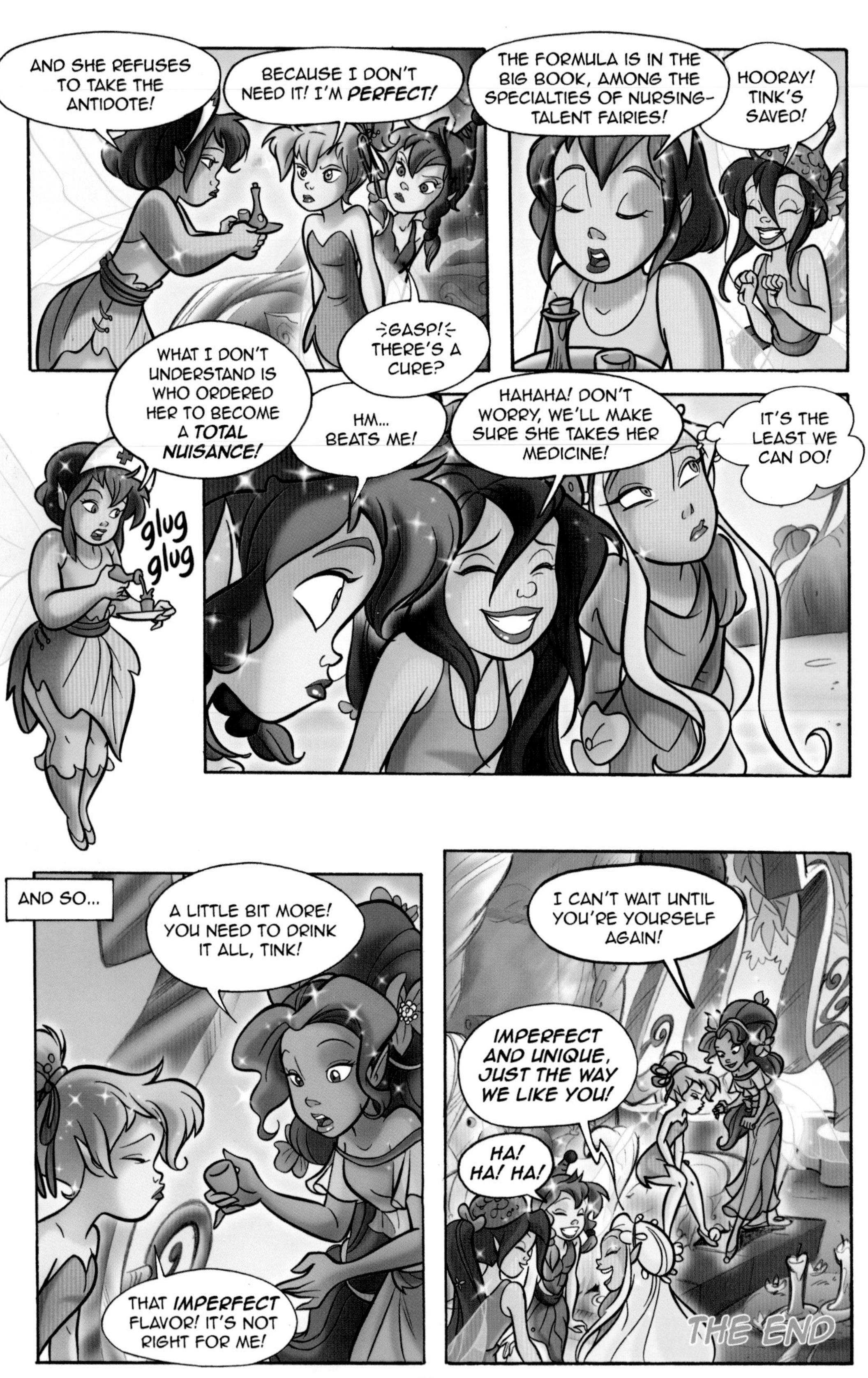
AND SHE REFUSES TO TAKE THE ANTIDOTE!
BECAUSE I DON'T NEED IT! I'M PERFECT!
THE FORMULA IS IN THE BIG BOOK, AMONG THE SPECIALTIES OF NURSING-TALENT FAIRIES!
HOORAY! TINK'S SAVED!
GASP! THERE'S A CURE?
WHAT I DON'T UNDERSTAND IS WHO ORDERED HER TO BECOME A TOTAL NUISANCE!
HM... BEATS ME!
HAHAHA! DON'T WORRY, WE'LL MAKE SURE SHE TAKES HER MEDICINE!
IT'S THE LEAST WE CAN DO!
glug glug
AND SO...
A LITTLE BIT MORE! YOU NEED TO DRINK IT ALL, TINK!
THAT IMPERFECT FLAVOR! IT'S NOT RIGHT FOR ME!
I CAN'T WAIT UNTIL YOU'RE YOURSELF AGAIN!
IMPERFECT AND UNIQUE, JUST THE WAY WE LIKE YOU!
HA! HA! HA!
THE END

WATCH OUT FOR
PAPERCUTZ™

Welcome to the seventh serendipitous DISNEY FAIRIES graphic novel from Papercutz. I'm Jim "the Sparrow Man" Salicrup, your award-winning[1] Papercutz Editor-in-Chief, and Pixie Dust Peddler!

We're all as proud as can be of this magical collection of DISNEY FAIRY tales—which features many moving and memorable moments. More than ever before we get to see Tinker Bell act all too humanly, even though she is a fairy. Her feelings are hurt when she doesn't win the cooking competition, yet she's conflicted when she has to judge the Fairy Fashion Show. She can't resist trying to change Vidia when the opportunity presents itself, yet when she tries to change herself and become the perfect fairy, she realizes that's impossible. (Yet, in her own way, to the millions of fans who love her just as she is—Tinker Bell really is "The Perfect Fairy.")

And if all that wasn't enough, we also had a super-special surprise guest—Peter Pan himself finally appears in the pages of a DISNEY FAIRIES graphic novel! If you thought his appearance was too brief, you'll be happy to know that he returns, along with Captain Hook, in DISNEY FAIRIES #8 "Tinker Bell and her Stories for a Rainy Day"! You don't want to miss it!

We also want to mention that if you enjoyed the beautiful artwork on "No Need for Words" and "Tink, the Perfect Fairy" that's probably because Antonello Dalena was one of the artists. If you like what you see, may I suggest another Papercutz series illustrated by Dalena that I'm sure you'll enjoy? It's called ERNEST & REBECCA, and it's the fun, and surprisingly touching tale, of a young girl and her best friend—who happens to be a germ! We think this new graphic novel series, available now at booksellers almost everywhere, is one of the best series being published in comics today! And a big part of that is the amazing artwork by Antonello Dalena—each and every page is filled with believable details, creating a world so real that you'll feel like you can step right into it! All I can say is that if you allow yourself to be exposed to ERNEST & REBECCA, the characters are so lovable, the humor so contagious—you won't be able to avoid being infected by them! (There's even a sneaky cameo appearance by a character we all love, as well as a zillion others, which makes looking at Dalena's artwork even more rewarding!)

(There's also another new series from Papercutz that Antonello Dalena and Manuela Razzi both illustrate. It's called SYBIL, and that's really all I can tell you about it—other that it's wonderful and magical and also available at better booksellers everywhere!)

Now that you know how much we love DISNEY FAIRIES #7— tell us what you think! You can e-mail me directly at salicrup@papercutz.com or you can send me an old-fashioned hand-written letter—just send it to Jim Salicrup, Papercutz, 40 Exchange Pl., Ste. 1308, New York, NY 10005. Or you can even visit us at www.papercutz.com.

So, until we meet again, don't forget to keep believing in "faith, trust, and pixie dust"!

Thanks,

Jim

[1] It's true! Jim won the 2011 CBG Fan Award for Favorite Editor! The Awards, sponsored by the Comics Buyer's Guide, and the voting is open to all comicbook fans. Jim thanks all the wonderful Papercutz writers, artists, colorists, letterers, designers, as well as Associate Editor Michael Petranek and Publisher Terry Nantier, for making him look good. And thanks everyone who voted for him as well—he greatly appreciates it.

Special Preview of DISNEY FAIRIES Graphic Novel #8 "Tinker Bell and her Stories for a Rainy Day"

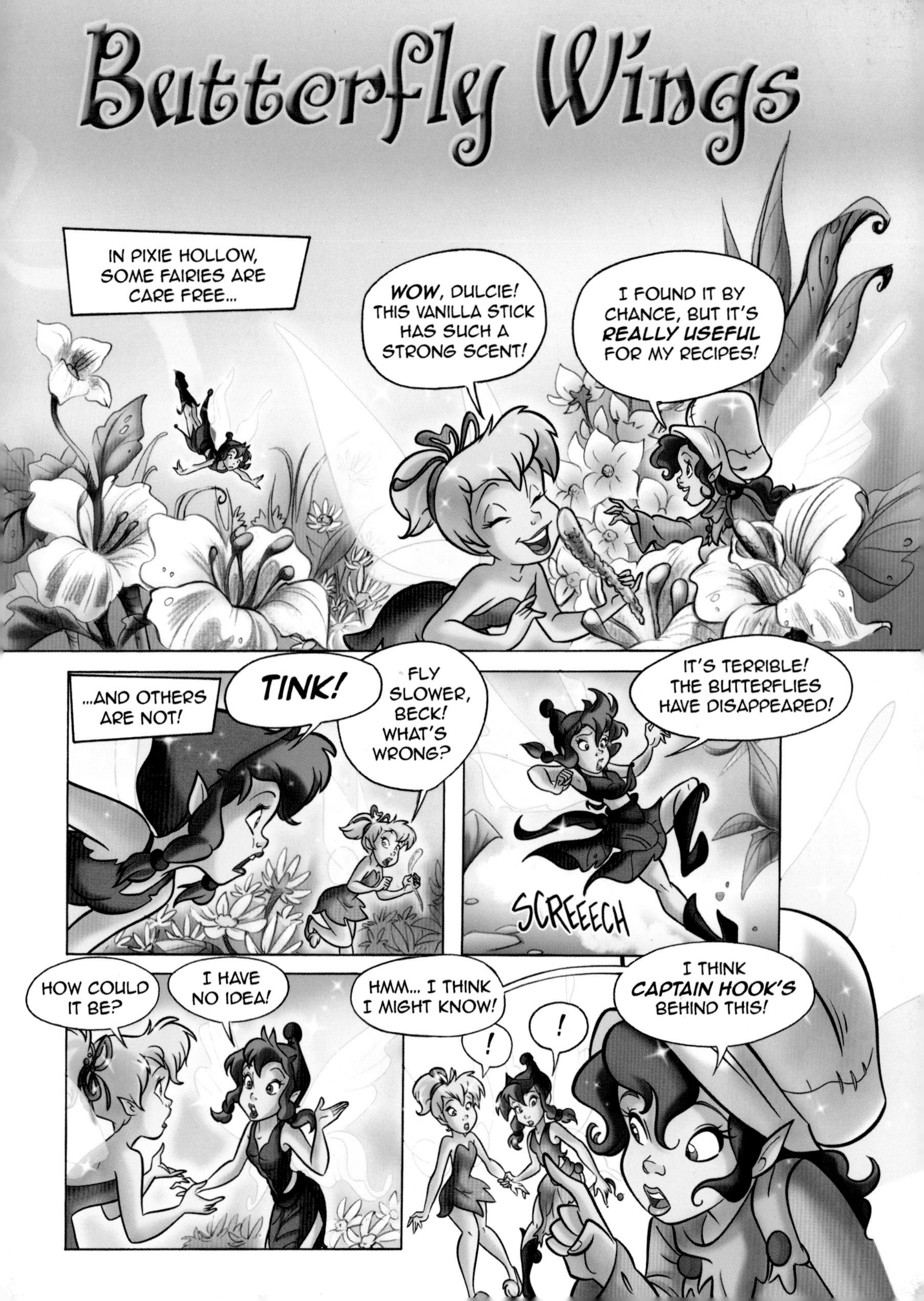
Butterfly Wings
IN PIXIE HOLLOW, SOME FAIRIES ARE CARE FREE...
WOW, DULCIE! THIS VANILLA STICK HAS SUCH A STRONG SCENT!
I FOUND IT BY CHANCE, BUT IT'S REALLY USEFUL FOR MY RECIPES!
...AND OTHERS ARE NOT!
TINK!
FLY SLOWER, BECK! WHAT'S WRONG?
IT'S TERRIBLE! THE BUTTERFLIES HAVE DISAPPEARED!
SCREEECH
HOW COULD IT BE?
I HAVE NO IDEA!
HMM... I THINK I MIGHT KNOW!
!
!
I THINK CAPTAIN HOOK'S BEHIND THIS!

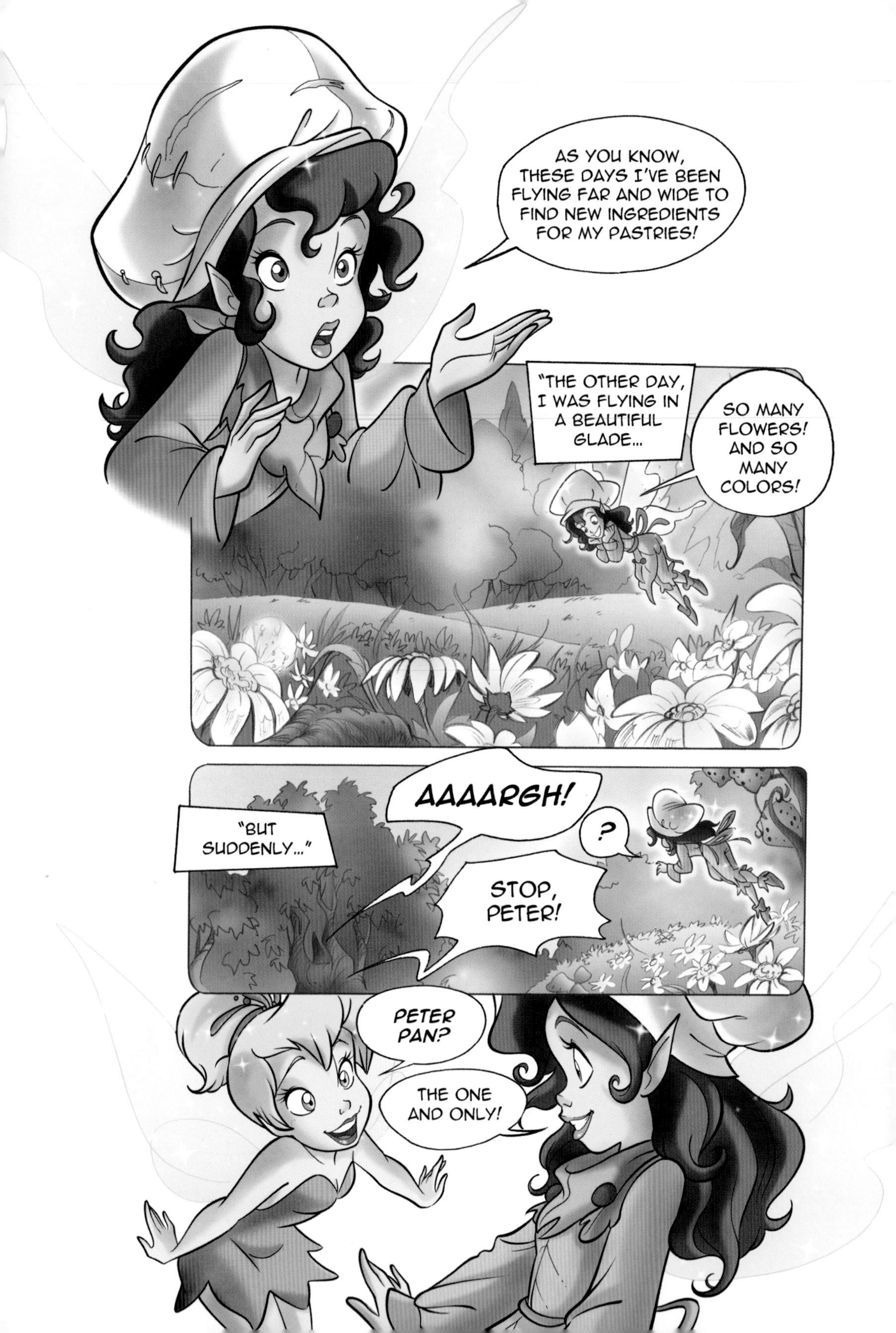
AS YOU KNOW, THESE DAYS I'VE BEEN FLYING FAR AND WIDE TO FIND NEW INGREDIENTS FOR MY PASTRIES!
"THE OTHER DAY, I WAS FLYING IN A BEAUTIFUL GLADE...
SO MANY FLOWERS! AND SO MANY COLORS!
"BUT SUDDENLY..."
AAAARGH!
?
STOP, PETER!
PETER PAN?
THE ONE AND ONLY!

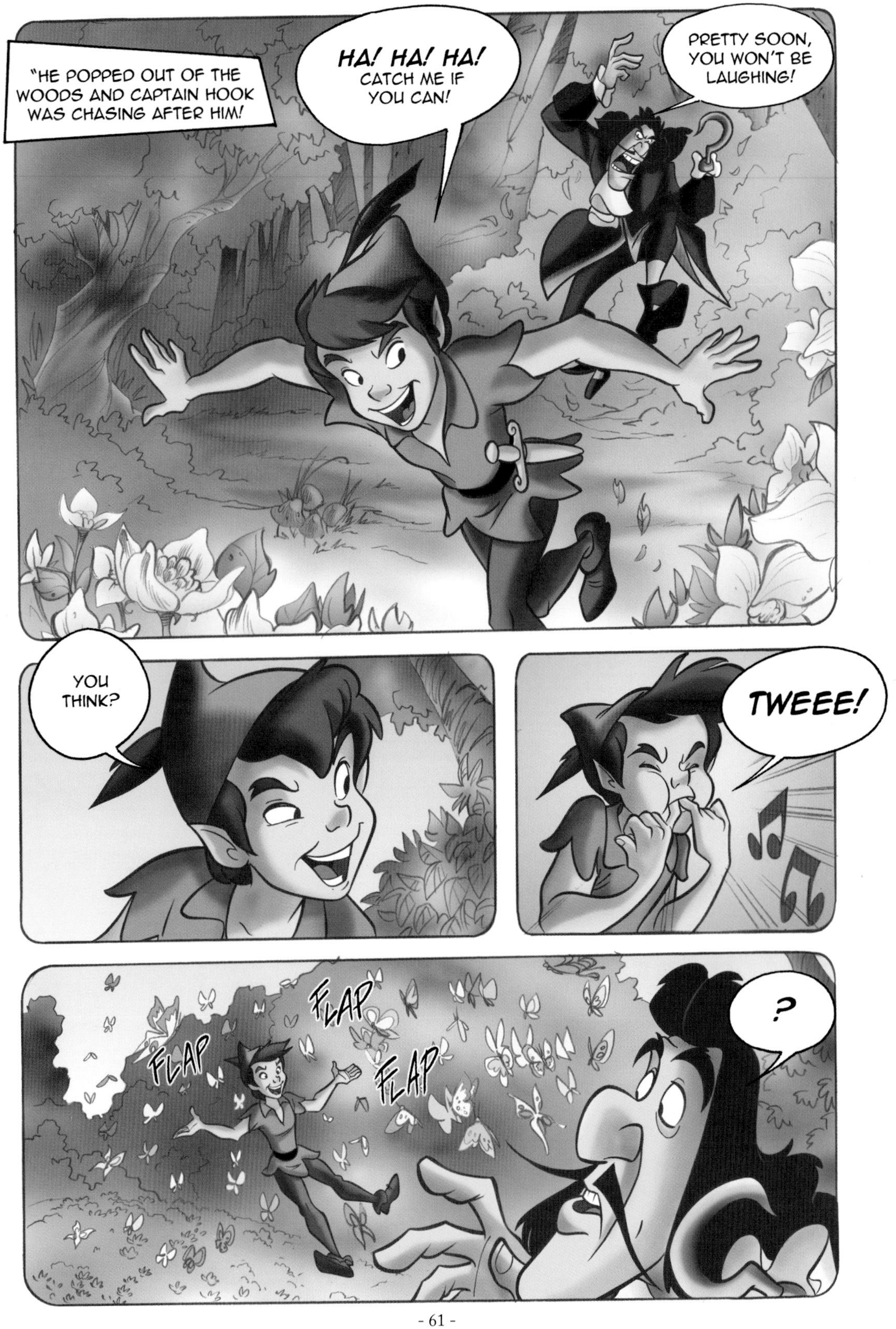
"HE POPPED OUT OF THE WOODS AND CAPTAIN HOOK WAS CHASING AFTER HIM!
HA! HA! HA! CATCH ME IF YOU CAN!
PRETTY SOON, YOU WON'T BE LAUGHING!
YOU THINK?
TWEEE!
FLAP
FLAP
FLAP
?

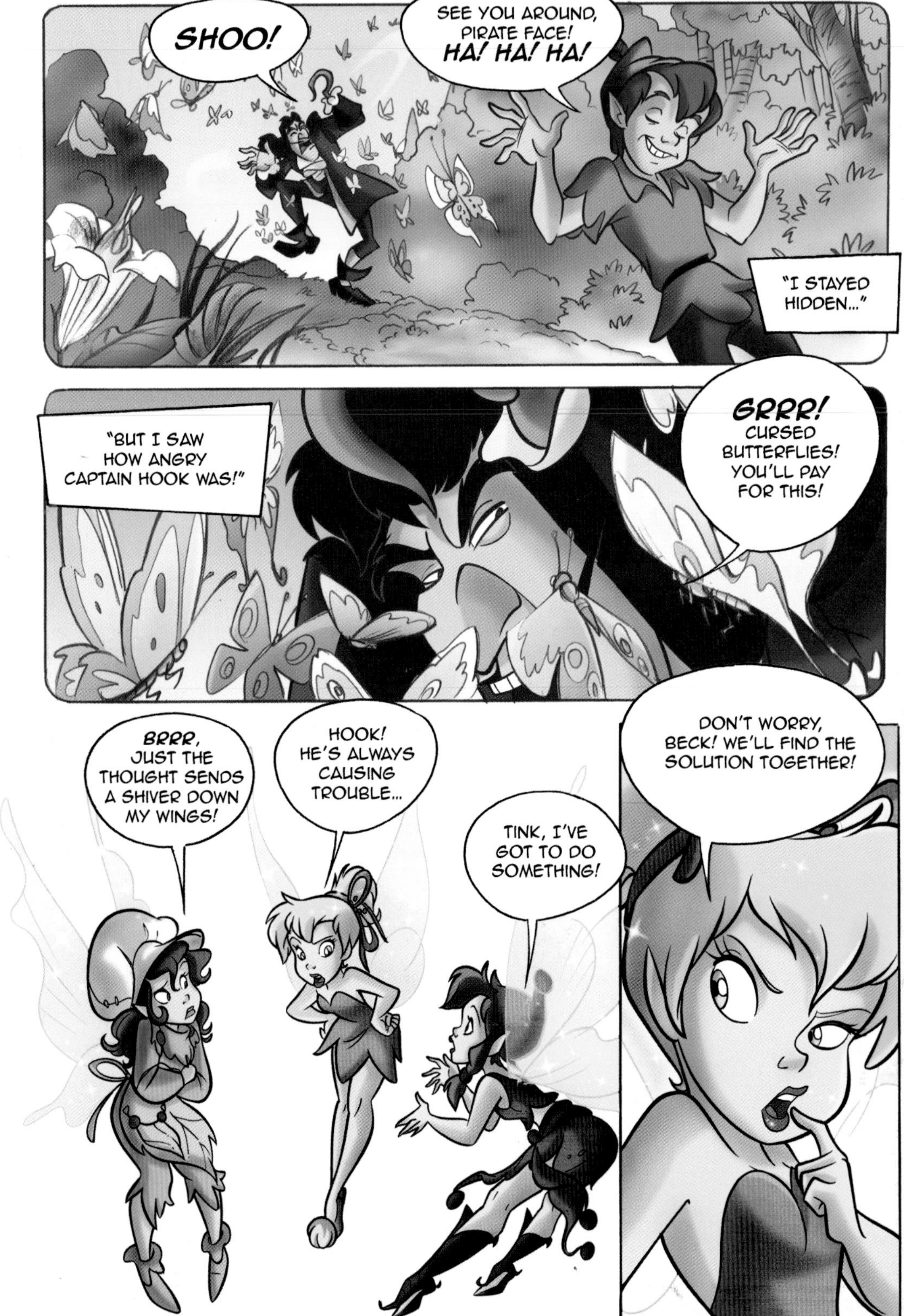
SHOO!
SEE YOU AROUND, PIRATE FACE! HA! HA! HA!
"I STAYED HIDDEN..."
"BUT I SAW HOW ANGRY CAPTAIN HOOK WAS!"
GRRR! CURSED BUTTERFLIES! YOU'LL PAY FOR THIS!
BRRR, JUST THE THOUGHT SENDS A SHIVER DOWN MY WINGS!
HOOK! HE'S ALWAYS CAUSING TROUBLE...
TINK, I'VE GOT TO DO SOMETHING!
DON'T WORRY, BECK! WE'LL FIND THE SOLUTION TOGETHER!

Disney fairies

Discover the stories of Tinker Bell and her fairy friends!

© Disney Enterprises, Inc.

COLLECT THEM ALL!

Available wherever
books are sold.
Also available on audio.